There had once been an age in which romantics could see men as natural wanderers, compelled to voyage from one stellar beacon to the next until they ran out of space or time—but there were no stars in the night skies over Orbitsville. Generations had come and gone without ever having their spirits troubled by the sight of distant suns. Orbitsville provided all the living space they and their descendants could ever need; Earth was remote and increasingly irrelevant, and there were better things to do with money than the propping up of ruins of forgotten cities. Madison, former administration center for the evacuation of seven states, was one of the few museum cities to remain viable, and even there funding and time were growing desperately short. . . .

ORBITSVILLE DEPARTURE

by

Bob Shaw

DAW BOOKS, INC.

DONALD A. WOLLHEIM, PUBLISHER

1633 Broadway, New York, NY 10019

DAW Collector's Book No. 622

First DAW Printing, April 1985

1 2 3 4 5 6 7 8 9

PRINTED IN U.S.A.

Chapter 1

They had decided to spend the few hours that remained to them walking in Garamond Park.

Dallen had been there several times before, but on this occasion his senses were heightened by a blend of excitement and apprehension. The sunlight was almost painful and colours seemed artificially intense. Beyond screens of trees the coppery roofs of the city shone with a spiky brilliance, and the nearby shrubs and flowers—gaudy as tropical plumage—seemed to burn in the sun's vertical rays. Lime-green lawns sloped down to the only feature of the scene which gave relief to the eye—a circular black lake roughly a kilometre across. Its nearer edge was obscured in part by low mounds of masonry and metal which were all that remained of an ancient fortification. Small groups of sightseers, their hats shifting ellipses of colour, sat among the ruined walls or wandered on the lake's perimeter path.

"Let's go down there and have a look," Dallen said to his wife, impulsively taking her arm.

Cona Dallen held back. "What's wrong? Can't you wait?"

"We're not going to start all that again, are we?" Dallen released her arm. "I thought we had agreed."

"It's all right for you to . . ." Cona paused, eyeing him sombrely, then in an abrupt change of mood she smiled and walked down the slope with him, slipping one arm around his waist. She was almost as tall as Dallen and they moved in easy unison. The feel of her body synchronising with his made him think of their prolonged session of love-making that morning. It occurred to him at once that she was deliberately working on him, reminding him of what he was giving up, and he felt a stirring of the resentment and frustration which had periodically marred their relationship for months. He repressed the emotions, making a resolution to get all he could from the hours they had left.

They reached the path, crossed it together and leaned on the safety rail which skirted the dark rim. Dallen, shading his eyes, stared down into the blackness and a moment later he was able to see the stars.

The surrounding brightness affected his vision to the extent that he could pick out only the principal star groupings, but he was immediately inspired with a primeval awe. He had lived all his life on the inner surface of the Orbitsville shell and therefore his only direct looks at the rest of the galaxy had come during his rare visits to this aperture. *When I get to Earth*, he told himself, marvelling, *I'll be able to drink my fill of stars every night . . .*

"I don't like this," Cona said. "I feel I'm going to fall through."

Dallen shook his head. "No danger. The diaphragm field is strong enough to take anybody's weight."

"Meaning?" She gave him a playful shunt with her hips. "Are you suggesting I'm too heavy?"

"Never!" Dallen gave his wife a warm glance, appreciating the good humour with which she faced her weight problems. She was fair-haired and had the kind of neat, absolutely regular features which are often associated with obesity. By careful dieting she had usually kept her weight within a few kilos of the ideal, but since the birth of their son three months earlier her struggle had been more difficult.

The thought of Mikel and of leaving him disturbed Dallen's moment of rapport. It had taken him the best part of a year to secure the transfer to Earth, with its consequent promotion to Grade IV officer in the Metagov civil service. Cona had been aware of his plans throughout her pregnancy, but not until after the birth had she revealed her determination to remain behind on Orbitsville. Her overt reason for not accompanying him had been that Mikel was too young for the journey and the drastic change of climate, but Dallen suspected otherwise and his pride was hurt. He knew she was reluctant to leave her ailing father, and also that—as a professional historian—she was deeply committed to her current book on Orbitsville's Judean settlements. The former had allowed no scope for recrimination, but the latter had been the source of many arguments which had been none the less corrosive for being disguised as rational discussion or banter. *Being Jewish is like a religion with some people . . .*

Something huge moved in the black depths below Dallen, startling him and causing Cona to jump backwards from the rail. After a second he identified it as

an interportal freighter slipping through space only
fifty metres or so beneath his feet, like a silent levia-
than swimming for the opposite shore of a black lake.
His gaze followed the ship until it was lost in the
mirages which overlay the more distant parts of the
diaphragm field. At the far side of the kilometre-wide
aperture was the space terminal where he would soon
embark for Earth. Its passenger buildings and warehouses were a dominant feature of the scene, even
though the principal installations—the giant docking
cradles for starships—projected downwards into the
void and were not readily visible.

"This place bothers me," Cona said. "Everything's
more natural in Bangor."

Dallen knew she was referring to the fact that their
home town of Bangor, 16,000 kilometres into Orbitsville's interior, was situated in Earth-like hilly terrain.
Its official altitude was close to a thousand metres,
which meant that amount of sedimentary rock had
accumulated there in the Orbitsville shell, but Dallen
understood that the geological structure counted for
little. Without the enclosing skin of ylem, the enigmatic material of which the vast sphere was formed,
the inner layer of rock, soil and vegetation would
quickly succumb to instabilities and fly apart. It was
an uneasy thought, but one which disturbed only
visitors and newly arrived settlers. Anybody who
had been born on Orbitsville had total faith in its
permanence, knew it to be more durable than mere
planets.

"We don't have to stay here," Dallen said. "We
could try the rose gardens."

"Not yet." Cona fingered the jewel-like recorder
which was clipped to her saffron blouse. "I'd like to

get some pictures of the Garamond monument. I might want to include one in the book."

You're supposed to be seeing me off—not working, Dallen objected inwardly, wondering if she had brought in the mention of the book to trigger precisely that reaction. Among the things which had attracted him to Cona in the first place was her independence, and he could see that he had no right to try changing the rules of their relationship. It was good that she was self-willed and self-reliant, but—the thought refused to be dismissed—how much *better* everything would have been had they been going to Earth together, sharing all the new experiences the journey had to offer.

There was, of course, an alternative to his present course, the alternative repeatedly put forward by Cona. All he had to do was delay his transfer by a couple of years, by which time Mikel would be bigger and stronger. Cona would have finished her book by then and would be mentally primed and prepared to enter an exciting new phase of her life.

Dallen was surprised by a sudden cool tingling on his spine. A radical idea was forming in his mind, thrilling him with its total unexpectedness. There was, he had just realised, still enough time in which to change his plans! He could get out of going to Earth merely by not showing up when the flight was called.

Bureaucratic though Metagov departments were, they all recognised and accepted one fact of human nature—that some people simply could not face the psychological rigours of interstellar travel. Backing down at the last minute and running away so commonplace that there was a slang term for it—the funk bunk—and no passenger's baggage was ever loaded until after he or she had gone aboard.

There was no shame in it, Dallen told himself. No shame in being flexible, in adapting to circumstances the way other people did. He had the opportunity to make a grand, romantic gesture of unselfishness, and there was no need to reveal to anybody, least of all to his wife, that it was actually a supremely selfish act in that it would enable him to hold on to what he cherished.

"Monument. Photograph." Cona wiggled her fingers close to his eyes. "Remember?"

"I'm with you," Dallen said bemusedly, trying to reassemble his internal model of the universe with different building blocks. He walked with Cona along the edge of the aperture to where the path widened into a small semi-circular plaza. Standing at its focus, on the very rim of space, was an heroic bronze of a man wearing a space suit of a design that had been in service two centuries earlier. He had taken off his helmet and was holding it in one hand while, with the other hand shading his eyes, he scanned the horizon. The statue was deservedly famous because its creator had captured a certain expression on the spaceman's face. It was a look of awe combined with peace and fulfilment which struck a responsive chord with all who had had the experience of climbing through an Orbitsville portal from the sterile blackness of space and receiving their first glimpse of the grassy infinites within.

A plaque at the foot of the statue said, simply: VANCE GARAMOND, EXPLORER.

Cona, who had never seen the monument before, said, "I must have a picture." She left Dallen's side and moved away among the knots of sightseers who were standing in the multi-lingual information beams being projected from the statue's base. Dallen, still lost in his own thoughts, advanced until a wash of coloured light flooding into his eyes told him that one of the roving beams had centred itself on his face. There was a barely perceptible delay while the projector studied his optical response to subliminal signals and correctedly deduced that his first language was English, then the presentation began.

Most of his field of view was suddenly occupied by images focused directly on to his retinas. They were of a triple-hulled starship, as seen from space, manoeuvring closer to a circular aperture in the Orbitsville shell. A voice which was neither male nor female spoke to Dallen.

It was almost two centuries ago—in the year 2096—that the first spaceship from Earth reached Optima Thule. That vessel was the Bissendorf, *part of a large fleet of exploratory ships owned and operated by Starflight Incorporated, the historic company which at that time had a monopoly of space travel. The* Bissendorf *was under the command of Captain Vance Garamond.*

You are now standing at the exact place where Captain Garamond, after forcing his way through the diaphragm field which retains our atmosphere, first set foot on the soil of Optima Thule . . .

The images were now a reconstruction of the first landing, showing Garamond and some of his crew on the virgin plain which was currently occupied by the sprawling expanse of Beachhead City. Relevant facts were murmured in Dallen's ears only to glance off the barriers of his preoccupation. What was to prevent him from actually *doing* it? What would it matter to the universe at large if he did not make the flight to Earth? There would be some fierce ribbing from the other pilot officers in the Boundaries Commission if he returned to his old job, but where were his personal priorities? What was the opinion of outsiders compared to the feelings and needs of his own wife? And there was three-month old Mikel . . .

The ruined fortifications visible to your right are among the few remaining traces of the Primer civilisation which flourished on Optima Thule some twenty thousand years ago. Although we know very little about the Primers, we can be sure they were a very energetic and ambitious race. Having discovered Optima Thule, they attempted to control the whole sphere—regardless of the fact that it has a usable land area equivalent to five billion Earths. To this end, they performed the incredible engineering feat of sealing with armour plate all but one of Optima Thule's 548 portals.

Opinions differ about whether they were vanquished by subsequent arrivals, or whether they were simply absorbed by the sheer vastness of the territories they had attempted to claim. However, one of the first actions of the Optima Thule Metagovernment was to order the unsealing of all the portals, thereby giving every nation on Earth unlimited and free access to . . .

Cartoon animations floated on the surface of Dallen's vision. Miniature ships were firing miniature radiation weapons, progressively clearing Orbitsville's triple band of portals, allowing the enclosed sun to spill more and more of its beckoning rays into the surrounding blackness of space.

The migrations from Earth began immediately, and continued at a high level of activity for a century and a half. In the beginning the journey took four months, but there came many rapid improvements in spaceship design which eventually cut transit time to a matter of days. At the height of the migrations more than ten million people a year were arriving at the equatorial portals, a transport undertaking of such magnitude that . . .

Annoyed by the intrusive voice and images, Dallen turned away sharply and broke the beam contact. He retreated to the curving edge of the plaza and sat down on a bench to watch Cona taking her holographic pictures of the monument. Again it seemed to him that her interest in the statue and its historic associations was a little too evident, that she was putting on a show for his benefit. The message was that she would be fully occupied in getting on with her own life while they were apart, but did he have to interpret that as defiance? Was it not possible, knowing Cona, that she was only trying to make things easier for him by not clinging on?

I'd be crazy to cut myself off from this, he thought, poised on the edge of a decision. He stood up and waved as Cona lowered her recorder and turned to look for him. She waved back and zigzagged towards him through the clusters of wide-brimmed hats which were worn almost universally on Orbitsville as protection from the sun's vertical rays. He smiled, trying to visualise how she was going to react to his momentous news. He had the choice of breaking it to her suddenly, going for maximum dramatic effect, or of a more oblique approach in which, perhaps, he would begin by suggesting that they go out of the hotel that night for a special celebration dinner.

Cona had just cleared the groups of sightseers when two boys of about ten ran up to her. She halted and, after a short exchange of words, opened her purse and gave them some money. The boys ran off immediately, laughing and pushing at each other as they went.

"Young monkeys," Cona said on reaching Dallen. "They said they needed carfare home, but you could see they were heading straight for the soda machines."

An inner voice pleaded with Dallen to ignore the incident, but he was unable to control his reaction. "So why did you give them the money?"

"They were just a couple of kids."

"That's precisely the point. They were just a couple of kids and you taught them it pays to ask strangers for hand-outs."

"For God's sake, Garry, try to relax." Cona's voice was lightly scornful. "It was only fifty cents."

"The amount doesn't come into it." Dallen stared hard at his wife, furious with her for the way she was casually destroying what had promised to be the most perfect moment of their lives. "Do you really think I give a damn whether it was fifty cents or fifty monits? Do you?"

"I didn't realise you were so hot on child welfare." Cona, standing within the vertical column of shade from her hat, might have retreated into a separate world.

"And what does that mean?" he asked, knowing exactly what it meant and challenging her to use Mikel as a weapon against him. They were standing on the edge of a precipice and the ground was breaking away beneath their feet, but the big drop might still be avoided if only she held back from using Mikel.

"This touching concern for strange kids," Cona

said. "It seems slightly out of place in a man who is about to jaunt off to Earth and leave his own son."

"I . . ." *I'm not going*, Dallen prompted himself. *Say it right now—I'm not going to Earth*. He strove to force the crucial words into being, but all human warmth had fled his soul. He turned away from his wife, sick with disappointment, locked in combat with the chill, haughty, inflexible side of his own nature, and knowing in advance that it was a battle he could never win.

Three hours later Dallen was on the observation gallery of the passenger ship *Runcorn* as it detached from the docking cradle and climbed away from the humbling and inconceivable vastness of the Orbitsville shell.

The ship was moving very slowly in the early stages of the flight, its magnetic scoop fields unable to gather much reaction mass in a region of space that had been well scoured by other vessels. As a consequence, the one-kilometre aperture around which Beachhead City was built remained visible for some thirty minutes, only gradually narrowing to become a bright ellipse and then a line of light which shortened and finally vanished. But even when the *Runcorn* was several thousand kilometres into space the inexperienced traveller could have been forgiven for thinking the ship had come to rest only a short distance "above" the shell. At that range Orbitsville was still only half of the visible universe, a seemingly flat surface which occupied a full 180° of the field of vision, the closest approximation in reality to the imagined infinite plane of the geometer.

Also, it was *black*.

Except in the vicinity of a portal, there was nothing to see when one looked in the direction of Orbitsville. There were no errant chinks of light, no reflections. As far as the evidence of the eye was concerned the familiar cosmos, which was so richly spangled with stars and galaxies and braids of glowing gas, had been sliced in half. There was a hemisphere of sparkling illumination and a hemisphere of darkness—and the latter was the stupendous, invisibly brooding presence that was Orbitsville. And even at a range of a billion kilometres, a distance which light itself took almost an hour to traverse, the sphere was awesome. It registered as a monstrous black hole which had eaten out the centre of the sky.

What, Dallen wondered, must the crew of the *Bissendorf* have thought when they were making that first approach all that time ago? What was going through their minds as they saw the edges of the dark circle balloon steadily outwards to occlude half the cosmos?

He could imagine those first explorers inclining to the idea that they had encountered a Dyson's Sphere. The 20th Century concept was that, in order to meet all its land and energy requirements, a highly advanced civilisation would eventually need to englobe its parent sun and spread across the inside of the sphere which had been created. A Dyson's Sphere, however, would have been a patchy and inconsistent construct, laboriously cobbled together over many millennia from dismantled planets, asteroids and cosmic debris. And it would have been leaking various kinds of radiation which would have given abundant clues about its true nature.

Orbitsville, in stark constrast, would have remained

enigmatic. Its shell of ylem was opaque to everything except gravitation, and therefore the wanderers of the *Bissendorf* would have known only that they were approaching a sun which had somehow been enclosed within a vast hollow sphere. Their long-range sensors would have told them that the surface of the globe was seamless and as smooth as finely machined steel, but no more information would have been forthcoming.

Even now, two centuries later, man's understanding of the sphere's origins was sharply limited, Dallen reminded himself. It was a study which had yielded little in the way of concrete fact, much in the way of speculation—a field which offered less to pragmatic researchers than to poets and mystics . . .

How does one account for a seamless globe of ultra-material with a circumference of a billion kilometres? There can be only one source for such an inconceivable quantity of shell material, and that is in the sun itself. Matter is energy, and energy is matter. Every active star hurls the equivalent of millions of tonnes a day of its own substance into space in the form of light and other radiations. But in the case of the Orbitsville sun—once known as Pengelly's Star—the Maker had set up a boundary, turning that energy back on itself, manipulating and modifying it, translating it into matter. With precise control over the most elemental forces of the universe, the maker created an impervious shell of exactly the sort of material He wanted—harder than diamond, immutable, eternal. When the sphere was complete, grown to the required thickness, He again dipped His hands into the font of energy and wrought fresh miracles, coating the interior of the sphere with soil and water and air. Organic acids, even complete cells and seeds, had been constructed in the same way, because at the ultimate level of reality there is no difference between a blade of grass and one of steel . . .

"Quite a spectacle, isn't it?" The speaker was a young woman who, unnoticed by Dallen had positioned herself beside him at the curving rail of the observation gallery. "It seems to pull your eyes."

"I know what you mean," he said, glancing down at her. The illumination was subdued, most of it from the extravagant blazing of star clouds, but he could see that she had Oriental features and was attractive in a forthright physical manner. He would have guessed she was an athlete or in some way connected with the performing arts.

"This is my first trip to Earth," she said. "How about you?"

"The same." Dallen was intrigued to find that, for one unsettling instant, he had been tempted to pose as a veteran space traveller. "This is all new to me."

"I noticed you coming on board."

Dallen weighed all the connotations of the remark, including her awareness of the fact that he was travelling alone. "You're very observant."

"Not really." The woman locked her gaze with his. "I only see what I like."

"In that case," Dallen said gently, "you're a very lucky person."

He turned away and left the gallery, easily putting the woman out of his thoughts. He was still angry with Cona, still feeling betrayed over their not making the trip as a family, but rebounding to another woman would have been a cheap and ordinary response, the sort of thing that many men would have done, but not Garry Dallen. His best plan, he decided, would be to make maximum use of the ship's gymnasium facilities, burn off his frustrations in sheer physical effort.

All the other passengers appeared to be tourists—couples, family units, clubs, study groups taking advantage of the heavy Metagov subsidy to visit the birthplace of their culture—and Dallen felt himself to be a conspicuoulsy solitary figure as he wound his way through them to fetch his training clothes. The gymnasium was empty when he got there and he went to work immediately, pitting his strength against the resistance frames, repeating the same exercise hundreds of times, aiming for a state of mental and bodily exhaustion which would guarantee his night's sleep.

His scheme was successful to the extent that he fell asleep within minutes of going to bed, but he awoke only two hours later with the depressing knowledge that it was going to be a long, uphill struggle to morning. He tried to pass the time by visualising his new job in Madison City, with all its opportunities for holiday travel to hundreds of fabulous old cities and scenic splendours so conveniently crowded on one tiny planet. But his brain refused to cooperate. No bright visions were forthcoming. As he drowsed through the small hours, in that uneasy margin between wakefulness and sleep where strange terrors prowl, Earth seemed an alien and inimical place.

And the doors of the future remained obstinately closed, denying him any hint of what was to come.

Chapter 2

Gerald Mathieu opened a drawer in his desk and, in spite of a drug-induced sense of *rightness*, he frowned as he looked down at the object within.

The gun was of a type which had once been known as a Luddite Special, and had been custom-designed for a single purpose—that of killing computers. It was also one of the most illegal devices that a citizen could own. Even with Mathieu's extensive connections it had taken him nearly a month to obtain the gun and to make sure that no other person in the whole continent knew it was in his hands.

Now the time had come to use it and he was highly apprehensive.

Merely being caught with the device in his possession would bring a mandatory prison sentence of ten years; and if it were established that he had actually used it he could expect to be removed from society for the rest of his life. The severity of the punishment was intended to protect people rather than property, because the weapon—in a consequence its inventors never foresaw—had a devastating effect on anyone caught in its beam. *In some ways worse than straigthforward murder*, had been one judicial comment, *and in many ways a greater threat to social order*.

"How in hell did I get into this situation?" Mathieu said to his empty office, then dismissed the question, trying to push irrelevancies aside as he picked up the gun and released the safety catch behind the trigger. The whole assemblage was solid and heavy in his hand, evidence of close-packed circuitry within, and a certain angularity and lack of cosmetic finish showed it to be the product of an underground workshop.

Aware that he was in danger of hesitating too long, Mathieu slipped the gun into the side pocket of his loose-fitting jacket and turned to check his appearance in a wall-mounted mirror. He had reached the rank of deputy mayor at the exceptionally early age of thirty-two, and he took a secret pleasure in seeming even younger by virtue of his fair-skinned athleticism. He also had a reputation for the casual perfection of his dress, and it was important that nothing about him should look out of place during the next few minutes. At this time of the morning his chances of encountering others on his way to Sublevel Three were slight, but the risk was always there and if a meeting occurred he wanted it to be unmemorable, something which would quickly be lost in City Hall's humdrum routine.

Satisfied that he had made himself ready, Mathieu went into the corridor and walked quickly towards the emergency stair on the building's north side. The transparent wall ahead of him provided panoramic views of the city of Madison. Its suburbs shone placidly in the distance, colours muted and outlines blurred

in the humid air streams swirling inland from the
Gulf. Mathieu, with a final glance back along the
empty corridor, opened the door to the stairwell and
went downwards. He had chosen to wear soft-soled
shoes and his progress was both swift and silent, like
the effortless sinking spiral of a gull.

Be careful, he thought, quelling a sudden exhilaration.
He had omitted his pre-breakfast shot of felicitin,
knowing he would need a clear head for the morning's
desperate venture, but the drug was bound to be
lingering in his system, subtly persuading him that
he was invincible. And a fall at this stage could turn
the threat of disaster into hard actuality.

The discovery some weeks earlier that Sublevel
Three housed an independent Department of Supply
computer had, in spite of the chemical shields around
his mind, numbed Mathieu with dread. It had been
installed decades ago at the instigation of some forgotten Metagovernment official, back in the days when
Orbitsville was more actively concerned with the affairs of Earth, and since then had—unknown to
Mathieu—been monitoring the distribution of certain
categories of imports.

The computer's specification had apparently been
drawn up by a bureaucratic supersnoop with a tendency to paranoia. It had an internal power supply
which was good for at least a century, and it obtained
its entire data input by direct sensing of product
identity tags within a radius of fifty kilometres. The
single feature of the system which had operated in
Mathieu's favour was that the computer did not inter-
act with Madison City's general information network.
It sat in the building's deserted lower levels, like a
spider interpreting every vibration of its web, acquir-

ing and storing detailed knowledge of the movement of Metagov supplies throughout the region. The information was jealously guarded, locked inside an armoured data bank—but it would be yielded on receipt of the correct command.

And even a cursory glance at the print-out would show that Mathieu had privately disposed of public property worth some half-a-million monits. The consequences of such a revelation were something that Mathieu could not bear to think about. He had resolved to destroy the evidence, regardless of the additional risk.

On reaching Sublevel Three he turned right and went through a ballroom-sized area which had once been used as a computer centre and now was a maze of movable partitions and discarded crates. He found the door he was seeking, one he would never have noticed under normal circumstances, and went through it into a short corridor which had three more doors on each side. The most distant bore the initials N.R.R.D. in stencilled lettering, a combination which meant nothing to Mathieu, and again he wondered how Solly Hume had chanced upon the troublesome computer in the first place. A junior architect in the City Surveyor's office, Hume was a self-styled "electronic archaeologist" in his spare time and was currently trying to have the machine declared obsolete and redundant so that he could buy it on behalf of some like-minded enthusiasts. It had been pure coincidence that Ezzati, the salvage officer, had mentioned the subject to Mathieu during a meeting, thus alerting him to the imminence of disaster.

Mathieu used his master key to open the door and quietly stepped into the fusty little room. The ceiling globe pinged faintly as it came on, throwing an arctic light over a plain metal table which supported the Department of Supply computer. It looked more like a strongbox than a complex electronic monitor, with only a plate engraved with chains of serial numbers to indicate its true nature. In a volume not much greater than that of a shoebox were sensors which could track the incredibly faint signals emitted by product identity tags, plus a computer which converted the signal variations into geographic locations and stored them in its memory. Millions of freight movements had been recorded, going back to before Mathieu's birth, but he was solely concerned with those of the last three years—the evidence of his grand larceny.

He stared at the box for a moment with resentment and grudging respect, and then—feeling oddly guilty— drew the Luddite Special out of his pocket.

He aimed its bell-shaped muzzle at the machine and squeezed the trigger.

Cona Dallen switched off her voice recorder, forced to acknowledge the fact that she was too hot and uncomfortable to do any serious work. She had chosen a seat beneath one of the mature dogwood trees in the City Hall grounds, but the shade meant little in the pervasive humid warmth. It was almost four months since she and Mikel had arrived from Orbitsville, and apparently she was no nearer to adapting to the climate of the area which had once been known as Georgia.

And being seven or eight kilos overweight doesn't help, she reminded herself, resolving to have nothing but green salad for the rest of the day. A glance at her watch showed there was more than an hour until the luncheon appointment with Garry. It seemed a pity not to do as planned and outline the next chapter of her book, but on top of the unsuitable working conditions she had a problem in that her subject was becoming increasingly remote.

With its working title of *The Second Diaspora*, the book should have been a genuine personal statement about the history of Judaism on Orbitsville, but—somewhat to her surprise—the work had gone slowly and badly after Garry's transfer to Earth. That fact had contributed to her agreeing to join him earlier than she had planned. Also, she had been touched when, trying to conceal his nervousness over venturing into academic realms, he had put forward the idea that distance would improve historical perspective. The prospect of ending a year of separation had helped persuade her he was right, that what she really needed was an overview, but now the two-century adventure that had been the founding of New Israel seemed oddly perfunctory, oddly passionless, when observed from a distance of hundreds of light years.

Was her new perspective valid? Was the fate of a single nation a truly insignificant fleck in the vast mosaic of history, or—as had been the case with other writers—had the very act of voyaging from one star to another leached some vital essence from her mind?

It was a mistake to come to Garry, she thought, and immediately regretted having allowed the thought to form. After four years of one-to-one marriage, it seemed that her relationship with Garry might turn out to be the durable armature around which she ought to build the rest of her life.

"Mum!" Mikel picked up the miniature toy truck he had been trundling through the grass and walked backwards until he was pressed against her knees.

"What's wrong, Mikel?"

He pointed apprehensively at a grey-and-white gull which had landed nearby. "A bee!"

"That's a bird, and it won't hurt you." Cona smiled as she clapped her hands and caused the incurious gull to retreat by several metres. To Mikel, every creature which flew was a bee and all four-legged animals were cats, and yet he had a vocabulary of at least a dozen nouns which he applied accurately to forms of mechanical transport. Cona wondered if a child could show engineering aptitude so early.

"Don't like," Mikel said. He continued to press against her and she detected the pure smell of baby perspiration in his coppery hair.

"It's too hot out here—let's go into Daddy's office and get a cold drink." She stood up, easily gathering Mikel into her arms, and walked towards the north side entrance of the City Hall. Garry's office would be empty till noon and, provided that Mikel was prepared to amuse himself unaided, offered a better environment for working.

The silvered glass doors parted automatically as she reached them, attracting Mikel's interest, and she walked into the air-conditioned coolness of the north lobby. Cona hesitated. The correct procedure would have been to go quarter-way round the building and report at the main entrance before taking an elevator to Garry's second-floor office, but her clothes were sticking to her skin, Mikel seemed heavier with each passing second, and there were no officials around to enforce the rules. Late morning stillness pervaded the lobby.

She opened the door to the emergency stair, a route favoured by Garry when he was in a hurry to get to work, and began the brief climb to the next floor, unconsciously making her footsteps as light as possible. There was a square landing midway between floors, and Cona had barely reached it when the air was filled with the shrill bleat of an alarm signal.

Shocked, filled with irrational guilt, she clutched her son closer to her and froze against the wall, momentarily unable to decide whether to turn back or go on.

The sound of the alarm caused Mathieu to moan aloud in panic.

He backed away from the Department of Supply monitor, knowing that the hail of radiation he had sent blasting through it would have erased programmes and memory alike. For an instant he thought the machine had retained the ability to warn of sabotage, then it dawned on him that there was a still-functioning alarm system somewhere in Sublevel Three, a relic of the days when it had housed a computer centre. This was something he had not even considered, yet another proof that it was foolhardy to plan anything important while under the influence of felicitin . . .

Why are you standing around? The words reverberated between his temples. *Run! RUN!*

He dragged open the door of the room and sprinted back the way he had come, moving so fast under adrenalin boost that he could actually hear the rush of air past his ears. His sponge-soled shoes made virtually no sound as he zigzagged through the huge outer room at dangerous speed. The continuing screech of the alarm lent super-human power to his legs as he reached the foot of the emergency stair and hurled himself up it in time-dilated dream-flight, taking four and five steps at each stride, his mouth agape and down-curved, scooping air.

I'm going to be all right, he thought as the floor markers appeared and dropped behind with impossible rapidity. *I'm going to get away with . . .*

The woman with the child in her arms appeared before him as in a vision. Time had now almost ceased for Mathieu. In an altered state of consciousness he recognised Cona Dallen, understood that she could and would destroy him, that she had no option but to destroy him, and in that protracted, tortured instant the weapon he was hardly aware of carrying came up level and his finger worked the trigger. A conical storm of radiation, noiseless and invisible, engulfed the woman and child.

Even before they had time to collapse, Mathieu had passed them, silently flitting upwards like a great bat, and the incident was part of his past. He reached the fourth floor landing, opened the door and saw that the length of corridor separating him from the sanctuary of his office was empty. Concealing the gun in a fold of his jacket, he forced himself to walk at normal speed until the blue trapezoid of the office door loomed large enough to receive him, then he turned the handle and went inside.

"It's not like murder," he whispered to the uncomprehending walls, again seeing Cona Dallen and her son go down before him, knowing with a bleak certainty that the scene would play itself behind his eyes forever in an endless loop of recrimination. "It's not a bit like murder."

Chapter 3

"I hate to tell you this, Garry, but it looks like we got a bandit in 1990 Street."

The voice from the transceiver in Dallen's ear came as an urgent, intimate whisper which shook him out of a reverie. Back on Orbitsville the idea of a three-year tour of duty on Earth had seemed valid, and not only because of the benefits to his promotion schedule. Earth, the home planet, had always had a romantic fascination for him, and working there was bound to give him a better opportunity to see it than any number of package tours. But the job was far from what he had expected, his wife was refusing to prolong her visit, and he had a yearning to be home again in Garamond City, breathing the diamond-pure air which rolled in from Orbitsville's endless savannahs. He was disconcerted by and ashamed of his homesickness, regarding it as an immature emotion, but it was with him all the time, only abating when something happened to break the daily routine . . .

"Are you sure about this?" he said, taking the

half-smoked pipe from his mouth and tapping it out on his heel. He was standing beside his car on Scottish Hill, a city park which gave extensive view's of Madison's southern and western suburbs. A brief rain shower had just passed over and he had been savouring the cleansed air. The museum section, which included 1990 Street, was less than four kilometres away and with unaided vision he could see the movement of traffic at some of its intersections, vapour-fuzzed glints of morning sun.

"Pretty sure," replied Jim Mellor, his senior deputy, who was on duty in the downtown operations centre. "Two of the new detectors picked up the remnants of a signal from a Lakes Arsenal product identity tag. Somebody has done his damndest to erase it, but enhancement of what's left indicates a TL37 fuze."

"That means a small bomb."

"Small enough to fit in your pocket—big enough to zap twenty or thirty people." Mellor quoted the figures without relish. "I don't like this, Garry. We've called in all patrols, but they're way out in the sticks and it's going to be twenty minutes before anybody shows."

"Tell them to come in low and quiet, and to land at least a kilometre away from the Street—if our visitor sees any fliers he's likely to pop his cork." Dallen was getting into his car as he spoke. "Can you tell which way he's heading?"

"He was sniffed out on the corner of Ninth, and then on Eighth. My guess is he'd heading for the Exhibition Centre itself. Going for the biggest number of casualties."

"Naturally." Cursing the scant Metagov funding which forced him to monitor the region with inadequate resources, Dallen switched on the car's pulse-magnet engine and drove down the hill towards 1990 Street. Rumours that a show-piece terrorist attack was imminent had been circulating for weeks, ever since he had intercepted a group coming up from Cordele and two of its members had died in the subsequent chase. He had given little regard to the stories, and even less to the refined versions which predicted an attempt on his own life, mainly because there was no special action he could take. His field force of sixteen officers was permanently overstretched, and now it looked as though a price might have to be paid.

Speaking without moving his lips, purely for the benefit of the transceiver in his ear, Dallen said, "Are there many tourists in the museum sector?"

"Not too many," Mellor replied. "Four or five hundred, and maybe a quarter of those are in the Exhibition Centre. Do you want me to start pulling them out?"

"No! That could trigger the crazy bastard off quicker than anything. Can you get a new fix on his position?"

"Sorry. There's practically no signal left in that fuze. It must have been a freak condition that let us pick it up on Eighth and Ninth, and I don't know if it'll happen anywhere else."

"Okay, but keep me posted—I'm going to walk up 1990 Street from the Centre and see if I can spot him."

There was a brief silence. "That's not part of your job, Garry."

"I'll give myself a reprimand later." The car's engine whined in protest as Dallen angled it down the hill in a series of high-speed swerves, cleaving occasional puddles into silver spray, using the full width of each street and jolting over sidewalk corners where necessary. His knowledge that there was little risk of colliding with another vehicle and none at all of harming pedestrians gave him licence to drive in a manner which would have been unthinkably reckless in normal surroundings. From the air, the Scottish Hill district looked like an ordinary suburb, but all its houses and stores had been empty for decades, sealed by near-invisible plastic skins which proofed their structures against decay. Most of Madison City was similarly deserted, similarly preserved, with time switches bringing on the street and house lights at dusk for the benefit of families who had long since emigrated to the Big O.

Reaching the edge of the museum district, Dallen turned the car into a cross-street and slowed down. He was less than a block away from 1990 Street itself and was entering the "living" sector of the permanent display. Solid images of cars and other vehicles—all of late 20th Century design—moved purposefully ahead of him, and seemingly real people in the costume of the period thronged the sidewalks and went in and out of stores.

The images had been closely packed to create an impression of overcrowded city life on Earth three centuries earlier, before the discovery of Orbitsville. Stationary cars formed a continuous line on each side of the street, apparently leaving no room for Dallen to park, but he knew the illusion was the least of his problems. He drove directly into a resplendent white Cadillac, unable to prevent himself flinching in the instant when the front of his own car burrowed into the convincingly real bodywork of the larger vehicle, and braked sharply. Sounds and smells of Madison circa 1990, accurately reproduced by hidden machines, enveloped him as he got out of the car and began walking north towards the next intersection.

"Garry! I think we just got another whisper near the corner of 1990 and Third." The voice in Dallen's ear now had a discernible edge of nervousness. "He's getting too near the Exhibition Centre."

"I'm on First, turning into 1990 two blocks east of him," Dallen responded. "Assuming we walk about the same speed, that means we should meet up near the corner of Second. It shouldn't be too hard to pick him out."

"Him or her."

"The masculine pronoun covers both genders— specially in this line of business." Aware that he had put too much effort into trying to sound pedantic and cool, Dallen brought his thinking into tighter focus. "Isn't the TL37 a dual-action fuze?"

"Yeah—timer and impact," Mellor confirmed. "That means if you don't immobilise him real fast he's liable. . ."

"I know what it means, Jim." Dallen negotiated the remaining distance to the intersection, stepping around the animated solid images as though they were real people, partly from instinct and also because there was a sprinkling of tourists in the simulated crowd. In most cases he could identify holiday-makers by the current fashions of their clothing, but some liked to dress in period for their venture into 1990 Street and it could be quite difficult to distinguish them from holomorphs.

He paused at the corner and took stock of his surroundings. A short distance to his right were the crystalline palisades of the Exhibition Centre; at successive intersections directly ahead were A.D.2090 Street and A.D.2190 Street, each a recreation of its own historical era; and to his left were the seething perspectives of a Madison City thoroughfare as it had looked three centuries earlier. And somewhere in that oppressive confusion of human beings and holomorphs there lurked a terrorist who was getting ready to ply his trade.

Dallen's confidence wavered as it came to him that he did not even know if his quarry was on the north or south side of the street. The images of the buses and commercial vehicles which jammed the central pavement were impenetrable to the eye, every bit as good as the real thing for providing an intruder with cover. Dallen slipped his right hand into the side pocket of his jacket and gripped the flat shape of his official sidearm. He rotated its beam control, setting the weapon to emit a broad fan of energy. It was unlikely that he would get enough time for precise marksmanship, and rather than miss his target altogether it would be better to bring down half-a-dozen bystanders and let them denounce him while they recovered in hospital.

"I'm walking east on 1990," he subvocalised. "If I reach the corner of Second without making contact I'm going to assume the bandit is either near me or has got past me. I'll wait thirty seconds then I'll say 'off'. As soon as I do that I want you to throw the switch and kill every image projector in the Street. That should take our visitor by surprise and give me a couple of seconds to pick him out."

"Okay, Garry," Mellor said, "but suppose there's more than one."

"It won't matter—I'm geared up to paralyse half the Street."

"I'm with you."

"Be glad you aren't." Dallen moved tentatively along the block, grateful that fashions in men's casual clothing had varied little over the centuries. His tan jacket, slacks and open-necked shirt made a virtually timeless ensemble which enabled him to mingle unobtrusively with tourists and holomorphs alike. He kept to the outer edge of the sidewalk, trying to scan both sides of the Street at once. His task was made a little easier by the fact that he could remember some of its permanent, though insubstantial, residents. There was the newspaper seller at the entrance to the Clarence Hotel, the amiably tubby guard at the bank, the cigar store owner who grinned his idealised grin at passers-by. Figures who paused and spoke to them, obeying their programmes, were immediately identifiable as holomorphs, as were taxi drivers, delivery men and the like.

Dallen's real problem lay with strolling window-shoppers and sightseers. A couple walking hand-in-hand with two small children were likely to be flesh-and-blood tourists, but similar family groups had been included in the Street's cast of holomorphs to establish a homely atmosphere—and there was nothing to stop bombers adopting the same camouflage. By the time he reached the midpoint in the block Dallen's palms were sweating and his heart rate had climbed until there was a continuous fluttering agitation in the centre of his chest.

He paused, striving to appear relaxed, and shielded his eyes from the sun. Business-suited men carrying leather briefcases hurried by him, a mailman with a

sackful of letters, a green-shirted youngster convers-
ing earnestly with a blonde in a pink dress, two
adolescents eating cotton candy, an elderly woman
laden with shopping bags . . .

This is hopeless, Dallen thought. *And it's funny the
way some people are making footprints and some aren't.*

Narrowing his eyes he picked out an area, some
twenty paces ahead, where rain from the recent shower
had accumulated in a depression in the sidewalk. The
sun had already dried the surrounding concrete, with
the result that people who walked through the shallow pool were leaving footprints for some distance on
each side of it.

*Except for the holomorphs, of course—illusions don't get
wet feet.* Dallen frowned, wondering why his heart-
beat had lapsed into powerful, measured anvil-blows.
There was nothing surprising nor even particularly
helpful about what he had noticed, and yet . . . and
yet . . . Lips moving silently, Dallen turned and ran a
few paces in the direction from which he had come,
giving himself a second look at one batch of pedestrians.
The crowd patterns had already changed, but he
found the couple he wanted immediately. The man
in the green shirt and the blonde woman were still
engaged in what had seemed to be a serious conversation, but—Dallen saw the pair with new eyes—only
the man was talking, and only the man was leaving
fast-fading smears of moisture on the sidewalk.

Dallen slowed abruptly, desperate for time in which
to devise tactics, but his erratic movements brought
him into near-collision with three women tourists in
holiday shorts. They made little sound, a barely audible gasp of surprise, but it was enough. The green-

shirted man glanced back at Dallen and began to run, dragging something from his hip pocket as he went.

Dallen hurled himself into pursuit, realised at once that another second was all the time the terrorist needed, and fired his sidearm through the material of his jacket. Several animated figures were caught in the cone of energy, but they were unaffected—holo-morphs—and Dallen ran clean through them as he glimpsed the bomber angling forward, rigid and toppling.

The fuze! The voice in Dallen's head had the hysteri-cal shrillness of a speeded-up recording. *How much impact will it stand?*

He overtook the falling man, clamped an arm around him and used the momentum of his charge to carry them both into the narrow entrance of an electronics store. Antique television sets in the glazed display areas on each side glimmered with images of an ear-lier age. A middle-aged couple who had been inspect-ing the television sets backed off in alarm, the woman pressing a hand to her throat.

"There's nothing to worry about," Dallen said, smiling a reassurance as he moved his right hand down the dead weight in his arms and gripped the metal cylinder which had been partially withdrawn from the bomber's pocket.

"Say, what's going . . . ?" The paunchy man broke off, looking doubtful, as the bomber made glottal clicking noises which indicated that his powers of speech would soon return. "Is that guy sick?"

Dallen weighed the alternatives open to him. The orthodox course would be to produce identification, send the couple on their way and call for assistance. But handling the situation that way, legally and properly, would have an inevitable consequence—a near-complete victory for the terrorist infiltrator. It was almost certain that the bomb's timing device was set to explode it within minutes, which left the authorities with the choice of evacuating the Street and allowing the destruction to take place, or of risking lives in an attempt to fly the bomb to open ground. Either way, the news would go out with tachyonic speed, the message that Madison City was no longer a safe place for visitors. Dallen looked down at the face of the young man he was cradling in spurious intimacy, saw the mute loathing in his eyes, and felt the bleak uncompromising side of his own nature respond in kind. He renewed his smile for the benefit of the watching people.

"Sick?" he said. "We should all afford to be so sick—young Joe here has just swallowed about a hundred monits' worth of happydust. He's got a habit of overdoing it."

The woman's powdery face registered concern mingled with distaste. "Will he be all right?"

"Right as rain, lady—it'll all come back up again any time now." Dallen eyed the couple ingenuously. "Can you lend me something to clean him up with? A handkerchief or a tissue or something." The sounds from the bomber's throat intensified, and Dallen patted his cheek with mock affection.

"Sorry . . . we're late . . . our friends are . . ." The man took his wife's arm and walked her back out to the sidewalk where they promptly moved out of sight.

Relieved to find that the incident had attracted no other spectators, Dallen transferred the cylindrical bomb to the safety of his own pocket, then manhandled the inert figure of his captive to the store's inner

door. It swung open as soon as he pressed his badge
to the lock. He quickly dragged his burden inside,
handling the large man with an ease which came
from regular strength training. The interior of the
store, apart from the window display area, was empty
and mouldering, a long cavern hung with cobwebs.
A dank toadstool-smell polluted the air. Heading for
a doorway at the far end, Dallen used the special
whisper which would be audible only at his headquarters.

"I've got him, Jim," he said. "We're in Cagle's
television store in the one hundred block, and there
was no fuss—so play everything quiet and cool. Send
a car to the rear of the premises, but tell the crew to
wait outside in the alley till I call for them."

Mellor spoke quickly. "What about the bomb?"

"It's going to be defused."

"Garry, you're not going to do something dumb,
are you? There's no way to neutralise a TL37."

There's one way, Dallen thought. "Radio reception is
pretty bad in here, Jim. Can you pick up my . . . ?"
He made the lateral movement of his jaw which
switched off the implanted transceiver, and—gouging
irregular channels in the silted dust of the floor—
dragged his captive into what had once been a square
office. There was a flurry of movement in one corner
as a grey shape disappeared into a hole in the skirting.
Dallen swung the young man into a sitting position
against a wall, pulled a billfold from the pocket of the
green shirt and scanned its contents.

"Derek H. Beaumont," he announced. "You should
have stayed at home in Cordele, young Derek."

"You . . . should . . ." Beaumont's mouth contorted

with the effort of speaking. "You should . . . go and . . ."

"Don't say it," Dallen cut in. "That sort of talk is very uninspired—certainly not worth losing your front teeth over." He took his first considered look at his prisoner and was relieved to find himself reacting with an instinctive dislike which was going to make his task easier. Some of the raiders he had come up against in the past had been personable youngsters, physical models he could have chosen for his own son, but the impression he got from the man before him now was one of arrogance and stupidity. Dilute grey eyes regarded him from a pale oval face which lost rather than gained individuality from a down-curving moustache. *The standard-issue Zapata moustache*, Dallen thought. *Or maybe they've only got one, and they pass it around.*

"You better not touch me," Beaumont said.

"I know—I've had hygiene lectures." Dallen took the cylindrical bomb from his pocket. "How many people were you hoping to kill with this?"

"You're the killer around here, Dallen."

"You know me?"

"I know you. We all know you." Beaumont's words were slurred as a result of his paralysis. "And one of these days . . ."

"Then you'll also know this isn't a bluff—you, young Derek, are going to tell me the combination for this." Dallen flicked the six numbered rings, close to one end of the cylinder, which would have to be correctly set to allow the fuze to be withdrawn.

Beaumont managed something close to a sneer. "Why the fuck should I?"

"I should have thought that was obvious," Dallen

said mildly. "You're going to be sitting on top of the bomb if it goes. How long have you got? Ten minutes? Fifteen?"

"You don't scare me, Dallen. You couldn't get away with a thing like that."

"Couldn't I?" Dallen thought for a moment about the effects of an explosion in the crowded Exhibition Centre and felt his humanity bleed away. "If you've got some dim ideas about publicity and propaganda—forget them. I hauled you way back here because a few walls and a good cushion of air are enough to contain a bomb this size. The bang will startle a lot of people, naturally, but they'll calm down when they hear it was one of the city's old gas mains. And *nobody* is going to hear about you, friend. This time tomorrow you'll be nothing but rat turds."

"You're a bastard, Dallen. You're a dirty . . ." Beaumont fell silent and the appearance of a thoughtful, introverted expression in his eyes showed that he was struggling to move, to force muscle commands across the artificially widened synaptic gaps of his nervous system. Lentils of perspiration appeared on his brow, but his limbs remained totally immobile.

"I'm everything you say, and more." Dallen knelt and held the bomb close to Beaumont's face. "What's the combination, Derek?"

"I . . . I don't have it."

"In that case, I'm sorry for you." The possibility that Beaumont was speaking the truth flickered in Dallen's mind, but he refused to consider it. "I'm going to get out of here now—in case this thing blows up sooner than we expect—but I want you to know I'll be thinking about you."

Beaumont's pallor intensified, making his face almost luminescent. "We're going to crucify you, Dallen. Not only you . . . your wife and kid, as well . . . just to let you see what it's like . . . I promise you it's all set up . . ."

"You've got a great talent for saying the wrong thing," Dallen said, keeping his voice steady in spite of the pounding tumult of his chest. "I don't want that combination any more. You can keep it—for a while."

He gently inserted the bomb at the juncture of Beaumont's thighs, making it a silver phallus, then straightened up and walked out of the room on legs that suddenly felt rubbery. *It's all gone wrong*, he accused himself, putting his back to the opposite side of the same partition that supported Beaumont and breathing deeply to overcome a developing sense of nausea. *I should have dumped the bloody bomb and hauled Beaumont outside and cleared the area. But now it's too late. It was too late as soon as he brought in Cona and Mikel . . .*

Taking his pipe from a side pocket, he filled it with black and yellow strands, and had put it in his mouth before realising he had no desire to smoke. All at once it seemed incredible, monstrous, that he was squandering the precious minutes of his life in such a fashion. How had he come to be trapped in the rotting carcase of a television store with a would-be murderer and a live bomb? Why was he confined to the claustrophobia and pettiness of Earth when he and his family should be soaring free on Orbitsville?

In the two centuries which had elapsed since Vance Garamond's discovery of Orbitsville the circumstance of mankind's existence had completely changed. One of the most quoted statistics connected with the Big

O was that it provided prime-quality living space equivalent to five billion Earths, but even more significant was the fact that it had enough room to accommodate every intelligent creature in the galaxy. For the first time in history there had been little or no brake on human expansion, and the migrations had begun immediately.

Earth's technology and industry had become totally absorbed in the last great challenge, that of transporting an entire planetary population across hundreds of light years to its ultimate home. It had been a venture only made feasible by two factors—the old world's declining birth rate, and the irresistibleness of Orbitsville's call. Every nation, every statelet, every political party, power group, religion, sect, church, family, individual could have the equivalent of a virgin world in which to pursue ideals and dreams. Governments had been slower to adapt to the new era than peoples, but statesmen and politicians—faced with the prospect of strutting empty stages—had eventually been persuaded that their duties lay elsewhere.

Each migratory government had, by UN agreement, retained responsibility for law and order in its historic territories, but time and distance had had their inevitable effect. Interest had declined, costs had increased, and many totalitarian states had in the end opted for the clean break solution, with compulsory migration of all subjects. Enforced migration to Orbitsville had not been possible in democratic countries, but that had not prevented governments—anxious to shake the clogging dust of the past from their feet—from using every conceivable inducement and pressure. More and more towns and cities had crumbled, ever larger areas of rural land had become overgrown, as the ordinary people had succumbed to the lure of the golden journey, the free trip to the Big O.

There had, of course, been those who refused to leave. Mostly they had been the very old, men and women who wanted to end their days on the planet of their birth, but there had also been a sprinkling of those who simply rejected the idea of pulling up stakes. And now in the year 2296, almost two hundred years after the finding of Orbitsville, the diehards in each area were still struggling to maintain a semblance of organised community life. But their situation had become less tenable with each passing decade as facilities had broken down and money and support from Orbitsville had dwindled . . .

"You're not fooling me, Dallen." The voice from the other side of the partition was confident. "I know you're out there, man."

Dallen remained quiet, tightening his lips.

"I'm telling you the God's truth, man—I don't have no combination."

You shouldn't have threatened my wife and boy. Dallen glanced at his watch, suddenly remembering he had arranged to meet Cona and Mikel for lunch, an appointment he was now bound to miss regardless of how things worked out with Beaumont. He would be unable to get a message to Cona unless he resumed radio contact with Jim Mellor, which conflicted with his resolve to claim all responsibility for his current actions. *It's all gone wrong*, he accused himself once more. *Why doesn't the moron give in before it's too late?*

There was a lengthy period of near-silence—the street sounds were murmurous and remote, part of another existence—then Beaumont spoke in less assertive tones. "What brought you here anyway, Dallen? Why didn't you stay on the Big O where you belong?"

Responding to the change in the other man's attitude, Dallen said, "It's my job."

"Hammering down on folk who's only standing up for their rights? Great job, man."

"They haven't any right to steal Metagov supplies and equipment."

"They *got* to steal the stuff if they can't afford to pay off Madison City officers on the quiet. Be straight with yourself, Dallen. Do you really think it's right for Metagov to keep a whole city going . . . a whole city lying empty except for a population of frigging optical illusions . . . while we got people sick and hungry on the outside?"

Dallen shook his head, even though Beaumont could not see, impatient with old arguments. "There's no need for anybody to go sick or hungry."

"I know," Beaumont said bitterly. "Let ourselves be rounded up like cattle! Let ourselves be shipped off to the Big O and turned out to pasture . . . Well, some of us just won't do it, Dallen. We're the Independents."

"Independents who feel entitled to be supported." Dallen was deliberately supercilious. "That's a serious contradiction in terms, young Derek."

"We don't want to be supported. We made a contribution too, but nobody . . . We just want . . . We . . ." Overwhelmed by incoherence, Beaumont paused and his laboured breathing was easily audible through the partition.

"And all *I* want is that combination," Dallen said. "Your time's running out."

He made his voice hard and certain, consciously

striking out against the ambivalence he usually felt when forced to think about Earth's recent past. Cona, as a professional historian, had the sort of mind which could cope with vast areas of complexity, confusion and conflict, whereas he yearned for a dawn-time simplicity which was never forthcoming. In the early years of the migrations, for example, nobody had planned actually to abandon the cities of the home world and let them sink into decay. There had been too big an investment in time. Mankind's very soul lingered in the masonry of the great conurbations, and hundreds of them—from York to New York, Paris to Peking—had been designated as cultural shrines, places to which Earth's children would return from time to time and reaffirm their humanity.

But the thinking had been wrong, bound by outdated parameters.

There had once been an age in which romantics could see men as natural wanderers, compelled to voyage from one stellar beacon to the next until they ran out of space or time—but there were no stars in the night skies of Orbitsville. Generations had come and gone without ever having their spirits troubled by the sight of distant suns. Orbitsville provided all the *lebensraum* thay and their descendants would ever need; Earth was remote and increasingly irrelevant, and there were better things to do with money than the propping up of ruins for forgotten cities. Madison, former administration centre for the evacuation of seven states, was one of the very few museum cities to remain viable, and even there funding and time were growing desperately short.

The thought of dwindling reserves of time prompted Dallen to look again at his watch. "I can't risk babysitting here any longer," he called out. "See you around!"

"You can't bluff me, Dallen."

"Wouldn't dream of trying." Dallen walked towards the front of the store, resisting the temptation to tread noisily on the dusty grey timbers of the floor. The slightest hint of overacting on his part was likely to strengthen Beaumont's resolve. As he dodged the insubstantial stalactites of cobwebs the conviction that he had made a mistake grew more intense and more unmanning. He decided to wait at the outer door for two minutes before dragging his prisoner out to safety, but new doubts had begun to gnaw at his confidence. What if Beaumont genuinely did not know the fuze combination or even the precise timer setting? What sort of justification could he give to others, to himself, if the bomb exploded and sent a blizzard of glass daggers through the pedestrians in 1990 Street?

On reaching the front door he leaned against the frame, pressing his forehead into his arm, and began the familiar exercise of catechising the stranger he had become. *What are you doing here? How long will it be before you—personally and deliberately—kill one of these sad, Earth-limited gawks? Why don't you pack in the sad, Earth-limited little job and take Cona and Mikel back to Orbitsville where you all belong?*

The last question was one which had confronted him with increasing frequency in recent months. It had never failed to produce feelings of anger and frustration, the helplessness which comes when a mind which likes answers is faced with the unanswerable, but all at once—standing there in the mouldered silence of the store—he realised that the difficulty lay within himself and always had done. The question was childishly simple, provided he faced up to and acknowledged the fact that he had made a mistake in coming to Earth. It was so easy. He—Garry Dallen, the man who was always right—had made a stupid mistake!

Aware that he was rushing psychological processes which could not be rushed, that he was bound to suffer reactions later, he posed the crucial question again and saw that it had become redundant. There was nothing under this or any other sun to prevent his taking his family home. They could be on their way within a week. Dallen, experiencing a sense of relief and release which was almost post-orgasmic, looked down at his hands and found they were trembling.

"Let's get the hell out of here," he whispered, turning towards the rear of the store.

"For Chris'sake, Dallen, come back!" The voice from the office enclosure was virtually unrecognisable, a high-pitched whine of panic. "This thing's set for 11.20! What time is it now?"

Dallen looked at his watch and saw there were four minutes in hand. At another time he would have walked slowly and silently back to the office, turning the screw on his prisoner to show him that life was easier on the right side of the law, but that kind of thinking now seemed petty. *Earth-limited*, was the term he had just invented. *I don't want to be Earth-limited any longer*.

He ran to the rear office, shouldered open the door and looked down at Beaumont, who was still unable to move. The silver obscenity of the bomb was projecting from his crotch. Suppressing a pang of shame,

Dallen retrieved the cylinder and fingered the fuze combination rings.

"You're going to be bastardin' sorry about this, you bastard," Beaumont ground out, his eyes white crescents of hatred.

"My watch might be slow," Dallen said pointedly. "Do you want out of here, or would you rather stay and . . . ?"

"Six-seven-nine-two-seven-nine."

"That must be a prime number." Dallen began aligning the digits with the datum mark. "Get it? Fuze—primer—prime?"

"Hurry up, for . . ."

"There we go!" Dallen withdrew the fuze and tossed it into a corner. "Thanks for your cooperation, Derek."

He left the office, walked along a short corridor to the rear of the premises and opened a heavy door whose hinges made snapping sounds as they broke bonds of rust. An unmarked car was waiting in the alley outside, its smooth haunches scattering oily needles of sunlight, and two young officers in uniform— Tandy and Ibbetson—were standing beside it. Dallen smiled as he saw the apprehension on their faces.

"Have a bomb," he said, slapping the cylinder into Ibbetson's palm. "It's okay—it's safe—and there's a character called Derek Beaumont to go with it. You'll find him resting inside, first door on the right."

"I wish you wouldn't do things like this," Ibbetson mumbled. His voice faded as he went through the door, turning his footballer's shoulders to facilitate entry, and lumbered along the corridor.

Vic Tandy, slate-jawed and meticulously neat, moved closer to Dallen. "Would you talk with Jim

Mellor? He's going crazy back there trying to reach you."

"He always does. Every time I get into a pocket of bad reception he . . ." Dallen broke off as he noticed Tandy's expression, oddly wooden and reserved. "Anything wrong?"

"All I heard is Jim wants you to contact him." Avoiding Dallen's gaze, Tandy tried to by-pass him and enter the building.

"Don't try that sort of thing on me," Dallen snapped, gripping the other man's upper arm. "Out with it!"

Tandy, now looking embarrassed, said, "I . . . I think something might have happened to your wife and boy."

Dallen stepped back from him, bemusedly shaking his head, filled with a sense that his surroundings and the blue dome of atmosphere and the universe beyond were imploding upon him.

Chapter 4

On the butt of the gun there was a stud which had to be depressed and moved from one end of a U-shaped slot to the other. It had been designed that way to ensure that the weapon, a highly expensive piece of engineering, could never be decommissioned by accident. Mathieu ran the stud along its full course, causing the myriad circuits to adopt new and permanent neutral configurations, then he stripped the gun down to four basic parts and hid them in separate drawers of his desk.

The action made him feel safer, but not much. His original plan, now revealed to have been woefully inadequate, had not allowed for a still-functioning alarm system on Sublevel Three, and he could only speculate about other possible deficiencies. The gun had been rendered invisible to any detectors the police might bring in, but there was no guarantee that an existing monitor had not already tracked its course through the building and into his office. If that were the case he would know about it very soon.

Behave normally in the meantime, he told himself, then came a question which was almost unanswerable to one in his state of mind. *What do normal people do when an alarm sounds?* He pondered it for a moment, like a man confronted by a problem in alien logic, and hesitantly reached towards his communications panel. The solid image of Vik Costain, personal assistant to Mayor Bryceland, appeared at the projection focus. Costain, who was close to sixty, made a profession out of knowing all there was to know about the City Hall and those who worked there.

"What's going on?" Mathieu said. "What was the racket?"

"Give me a break, will you? I'm still trying to . . ." Costain tilted his near-hairless head, obviously listening to an important message, and nodded decisively—a sure sign he had no idea what to do next. "Call me later, Gerald."

"Don't forget to let me know if the building's on fire," Mathieu replied, breaking the connection. He breathed deeply and regularly for a minute, satisfied that he had put on a reasonable act, gone some distance towards covering his tracks, then he closed his eyes and saw Cona Dallen and her son falling . . . falling and folding . . . their eyes already bright and incurious . . . idiot eyes . . .

Mathieu leaped to his feet and walked around the perimeter of his office, suddenly unable to dredge enough oxygen from the air. He had made the circuit a second time, faster, before realising he was trying to outrace a part of himself, the part which acknowledged that he—Gerald Mathieu—was a murderer. No amount of sidestepping or playing with definitions was going to change that fact. Continuance of personality was the sole criterion, the only one which counted, and the personalities known as Cona Dallen and Mikel Dallen no longer existed. He had blasted them away in a storm of complex radiations which had returned two human brains to the tabula rasa condition of the newborn infant, and those personalities would never exist again, no matter what therapies were employed.

Garry Dallen will kill me! Mathieu abruptly stopped walking and pinched the bridge of his nose between finger and thumb, trying to come to terms with the new thought. There was little that was fanciful or melodramatic about it. Dallen was a big, powerfully built, handsome man who worked a little too hard at appearing casual, who was always a little too quick with the joke or pleasantry designed to put those about him at their ease. Mathieu, a gifted people-watcher, had privately sized him up as inflexible and intolerant, with the capacity to be ruthless in pursuit of what he believed to be right. He had always been afraid of Dallen, even when there was nothing more than well-concealed graft on his conscience—now he had a chilling conviction that Dallen would look straight into his soul, know him for what he was, and come after him like a remorseless machine.

"No more than you deserve," he said, addressing his image in a wall mirror he had had specially installed. The man he saw looked surprisingly relaxed and confident, like a Nordic tennis champion on holiday, giving no indication of criminality or of the hunger which was growing more insistent in him by the minute. The thought of felicitin caused Mathieu to slip a hand into his jacket and touch the gold pen clipped in the inner pocket. It was a functional writing instrument, but with a small adjustment it dispensed a magical ink. A one-centimetre line drawn on the tongue was enough to put right everything that was wrong in Mathieu's life, not only for the present but working in retrospect, right back to the time he had come from Orbitsville at the age of eight.

His father, Arthur Mathieu, had been a minor Metagov official who had followed the promotion trail to Earth and had lost his way in a maze of gin bottles and ill-starred departmental shuffles. The community of government workers in Madison City was small and close-knit, and the boy Gerald—humiliated by his father's failure—had gone through school as a solitary stroller, barely achieving grades, dreaming of the day he would return to the Big O's delicately ribbed sky and up-curving horizons. Then, when Gerald was sixteen, his father had died in a ludicrous accident involving a hedge trimmer, and suddenly the way back had been open. His mother was returning, his younger sister was returning, but Mathieu had found he was afraid of the return journey and even more terrified of Orbitsville itself. He had claimed the right to an unbroken education and by sheer force of belated effort had built a successful career in Madison, achieving a position which no reasonable person would expect him to quit merely to return to his boyhood home.

Mathieu understood his own private strategy, however. And although one part of his mind assured him his timidity was of no consequence—another part, brooding and illogical, saw it a serious character defect, evidence of a void where there should have been the cornerstone of a personality. He had tried psychological judo, presenting his weaknesses as cute

foibles. *I've never had the slightest trace of will power—
ask anybody who knows me. There is only one way to get
rid of temptation—give in immediately. You can always
trust me to let you down . . .*

Then had come felicitin, bringer of the ultimate
high. Felicitin, which could have been custom-designed
by a master chemist for Mathieu's personal salvation,
which made the user feel not only good, but *right*.
Felicitin, at five thousand monits and more for an
amount the size of a single teardrop.

For which he had become a thief.

For which he had become a murderer.

Mathieu drew the gold pen out of his pocket,
clenched both hands around it and made as if to snap
it in two. He stood that way for a full minute,
changing his grip on the cylinder several times,
trembling like a marksman afflicted with target-shyness,
then his posture relaxed as he felt himself arrive at
one of his rationalisations. There was no need to try
kicking the habit. Dallen would be quick to ascertain
the events leading to the annihilation of his family,
to leap from motive and opportunity to half-intuitive
identification. Soon after that Mathieu would be going
to the prison colony—if Dallen let him get that far—
and in prison one did not have to struggle to escape
drug dependency. The cold turkey treatment was
thrown in free with the uniform and the rehab tapes.

From beyond his door there came the sound of
other doors slamming, excited voices, rapid footsteps.
One thing which had not changed over the centuries
was the essential dullness of most administrative jobs,
and on a heavy summer's morning, with the outside
world shimmering on the windows like a multicoloured
dream, the sense of ennui in the corridors was almost

tangible. Now something out of the ordinary had happened in the building and the word was going around. This was going to be a day to remember.

Mathieu slipped his pen back into his pocket, sat down at his desk and tried to plan the next hour. He decided, having made his for-the-record enquiry, to wait where he was until someone requested his presence downstairs. Frank Bryceland, the mayor, was out of town for two days, so it was likely that Mathieu would be summoned as soon as Costain realised what had happened. As the minutes slowly filtered from future into past he felt mildly surprised at how long Costain was taking, then he began to appreciate the variance between his own informed viewpoint and those of other people in the building. An alarm had sounded without any immediately identifiable cause; a security check could be slow and tentative; and the condition of the woman and child lying on the emergency stair might take time to diagnose, especially as Luddite Specials were far from common by the end of the 23rd Century.

Prompted by impulse, Mathieu went to the window and looked down at the north side car park just as a police cruiser came slewing in from Burlington Avenue. As soon as it had stopped three men got out and ran towards the north lobby. Something gave an icy heave in Mathieu's stomach as he recognised the black-haired figure of Garry Dallen loping along with unconscious power, looking as though he could run clear through the wall of the building. Feeling cold and isolated, Mathieu returned to his desk and sat staring at his hands, waiting.

Perhaps five minutes had gone by before there was a chiming sound and Costain's head hovered before him. Errant flecks of light swarming like fireflies around the image showed the projector was losing its adjustments.

"Can you come down to the north lobby?" Costain sounded both nervous and guarded. "Right now?"

"What's the matter?"

"It looks like somebody has wiped Cona Dallen and her boy."

"*Wiped* them!" Mathieu conveyed puzzlement. "Do you mean . . ?"

"Yeah—total brain scour. Didn't you know?"

"No, I . . ." Mathieu paused, sensitive to the question. "How the hell would *I* know? I've been sitting in my . . ."

Costain shook his head. "It's all over the building, Gerald. You'll have to make a statement."

"I'm on my way down." Mathieu stood up as Costain's image dissolved. He went to the door, smoothing his hair and making slight adjustments to the hang of his jacket. It was important for him to look his best when going into a difficult situation, and facing up to Dallen was going to be the worst ever, the ultimate bad scene. The elevator was waiting, and with almost no lapse of time he was in the lobby, working his way through barriers of people, all of whom were facing the door of a room which had once been used by commissionaires, back in the days when Madison had been booming. Vik Costain, as though telepathically forewarned, opened the door as Mathieu reached it, quickly drew him inside and clicked the lock.

"We're all going to roast over this one," Costain said, the folds of his grey face set like rippled lava. "Frank has been griping about security for months."

"I know," Mathieu mumbled, moving further into the room to become part of its central tableau. Cona Dallen was stretched out on her back on the floor, hands making random little pawing movements in the air. Her lightweight saffron dress was in disarray, showing her conical thighs, but the display was asexual because her face was blank and serene, unmarked by identity, and her eyes were those of a baby—bright, humorous, uncomprehending. A bubbled ribbon of saliva ran from one corner of her mouth. Garry Dallen was kneeling beside her, rocking gently with his son gathered in his arms, his face hidden in the boy's hair. Mathieu said a silent farewell to joy.

Costain touched Mathieu's arm. "Who would do a thing like this?"

"I know who did it," Dallen announced in a leaden, abstracted voice. He raised his head and slowly looked around the half-dozen men in the room. Mathieu's heart juddered to a standstill as the grey, tear-lensed eyes locked with is own, but—miraculously—Dallen's gaze wandered away from him without pause. It was as if they had become strangers.

"I did this," Dallen continued.

One of the policemen in the group moved uneasily. "Garry, I don't think you should . . ."

Dallen silenced him with a look. "I brought my family to this place . . . I handled the job wrong . . . pushed too hard . . . ignored the threats . . ." A muscular spasm pulled his mouth downwards at the corners, producing a caricature of an urchin who had just been thrashed, and when he spoke each word was the snapping of a glass rod. "Why couldn't I have been with them? I don't *deserve* a brain . . ."

"I'm going to see what's holding the ambulance," Costain said, striding to the door.

"Good idea." Mathieu went through the doorway on the heels of the older man, anxious to leave the emotional autoclave of the room. Instead of following Costain to the lobby's outer doors he turned right along the corridor and went into a washroom. It was cool and empty, heavily perfumed with soap. In the furtive privacy of a cubicle he took the gold pen from his pocket, reset the point and drew it across his tongue, making a line twice as long as was usual for him.

I might be lucky, he thought. *Perhaps I'm going to get away with it.*

He closed his eyes retreating inwards, waiting for chemical absolution.

Chapter 5

The accident occurred about eighty minutes into the flight.

Jean Antony's first intimation that something serious was happening came when instrumentation panels began to go dead without any accompanying warning signals. Her Type 83 freighter was more than a century old and some of its systems were afflicted with a kind of electronic gangrene, but the fault indicator circuits were supposed to be in good shape. The fact that some had failed could be trivial or catastrophic. She knew it could involve as little as an annoying extra maintenance charge, or as much as . . .

Dear God! The prayer was instinctive, unconnected with religious belief. *Dear God, don't let this cargo kill me.*

The ship's antiquated ion thrusters were creating only a fifth of normal gravity, enabling Jean to cross the control gallery in one floating stride. She glanced at the master status indicator—an array of glowing

block diagrams, most of them in the form of longitudi-
nal sections through the hull—and saw a spreading
blackness which could only mean that a Bessemon-D
container had ruptured in the cargo hold. For a moment she allowed herself to feel shocked at the sheer
unfairness of what had happened, a series of suppos-
edly perfect fail-safe devices failing so dangerously,
then came the realisation that she was lingering in a
spacecraft which could literally be dissolving around
her.

Bessemon-D was a solvent gas which had displaced
nine-tenths of the capital equipment traditionally associated with metal foundries. In normal circumstances
it was inimical life, but drifting free within a spacecraft it was capable of ending Jean Antony's existence
in a dozen different ways. Destruction of the pressure hull was the obvious danger, but for all she
knew the first lethal wisps could already be swirling
towards her through ventilation ducts, speeded on
their way by plastic impellers. There was no time to
waste.

"Code Zero-zero-one!" she shouted as she hurled
herself towards the emergency capsule compartment.
No acknowledgement came from the on-board computer. As she opened the door to the compartment
most of the lights on the control panel began to
flicker and a sudden queasiness in her stomach told
her the ship's thrust controllers were behaving errati-
cally. She stepped into the capsule and allowed the
door to slam and seal behind her. A shuddering
unlike anything she had previously encountered in
twenty years of astrogation stirred the capsule into
life, bringing with it the conviction that it was too
late to escape whatever fate was overtaking the mother

ship. The capsule's activator button sprang into ruby brilliance, splintering the claustrophobic darkness.

Jean hit the button with the heel of her right hand. There was an explosion, a wrenching jolt and a second later she was adrift in space, only fifty kilometres above the inconceivable vastness of Orbitsville.

Jean's first reflexive action was to check that the capsule's radio beacon was functioning properly. She located the pulsing green rectangle on the miniature instrument panel, touched it for reassurance, then raised her eyes to see how the doomed freighter was faring. The coffin-sized capsule had all-round visibility, and from its viewpoint the universe was divided into two equal parts. "Above" was a hemisphere of stars, many of them individually brilliant against fainter swarms and the frozen luminous clouds of the Milky Way; "below" there appeared to be nothing.

In spite of her years of plying the two-hundred-plus equatorial portals, Jean's brain still tended to interpret the scene as though she were in a low-flying plane which was skimming the surface of a dark ocean. She scanned the region directly below the capsule, expecting to pick out the lights of the freighter at once, and was surprised and only faintly alarmed to observe unbroken night. Did it mean that every power source on the ship had failed, dousing even the astrogation lights?

That can't be, she told herself. *Not so soon.*

She frowned, still puzzled rather than worried, turning her head from side to side to take in larger areas of the blackness below her. Then, from a corner of her eye, she became aware of something huge occulting the star fields above her. She twisted around in the confined space and verified what the first intuitive shock had already told her—that the opaque mass was the freighter sliding ahead on its own course.

Refusing to allow herself to panic, Jean studied the larger vessel and tried to decide what had gone wrong with the escape. The answer came quickly. Astrogation and marker lights were slipping across the long silhouette at increasing speed, which meant that the disfunction of its thrust controllers had caused the ship to rotate. And instead of the capsule having been ejected upwards, to carry it into space and clear of the equatorial trade lanes, it had been fired downwards in the direction of Orbitsville. She was bound for a grazing collision with the unseen surface a mere fifty kilometres below.

Until that moment Jean's principal concern had been the loss of the *Atkinson Grimshaw*, the old ship—named after a favourite Victorian artist—which was on the point of annihilating both itself and most of her assets. With the skimpiness of her insurance coverage, the incident probably meant the end of the one-woman transport business she had been operating for eight years, ever since her mother had died, but now such considerations were trivial. The capsule was travelling downwards at about forty kilometres an hour, and also had a forward component of about thirty thousand—the speed at which it had parted company with the ship. These velocities, relative to the Orbitsville shell, were small compared to normal operational speeds, but they were enough to destroy the thin-walled capsule in the collision which was due in approximately seventy-five minutes.

Life or death, for her, had become a question of how long it would take the rescue services to react.

At the age of forty, Jean had retained the instinctive belief in immortality which comes from good health, good looks, an active intelligence and a satisfying life style. But now, floating in silence above the invisible vastness of the Big O's outer surface, she had to weigh up the chances of surviving the day, knowing in advance that the odds were not in her favour.

Orbitsville had three bands of circular portals—one at its equator, one in each of the northern and southern hemispheres. Those on the equator, spaced at intervals of roughly five-million kilometres, had been given the identification numbers 1 to 207, counting east from the portal which had first been penetrated by Vance Garamond and the crew of his SEA flickerwing. Thriving ports and cities had subsequently sprung up around many of the entrances during the great migrations from Earth, and at that time the equatorial trade lanes had been busy and well regulated. But those cities had been built almost from force of habit, dying manifestations of mankind's need for safe huddling places. With unlimited territory available there was no longer any need for competition, conflict or defence. The millions from Earth had been effortlessly absorbed, lured by Orbitsville's endless savannahs, and—as quickly as they were created—many cities had been abandoned, echoing the fate of their forebears on the home world.

During Jean's career the interportal space traffic had dwindled drastically, and therein lay the threat to her life. She had been flying east from 156 to another still-viable industrial centre at 183. Eighty minutes into the flight she was, as a consequence of the freighter's puny acceleration, only twenty-thousand

kilometres from her starting point, and in the old
days would quickly have been reached by the high-
performance patrol vessels monitoring the traffic around
each portal. In the last decade of the 23rd Century,
however, the emergency services had been pared down
to the minimum and in any case were accustomed to
the leisurely type of recovery mission which would
have been effective had Jean been ejected upwards.
She had a conviction that nobody would even notice
anything unusual about her distress signal until it
was too late.

She stared down into the featureless blackness and
tried to see it as an incredibly hard wall which was
rushing upwards with deadly speed. The air circulating around her smelled strongly of rubber and plastics,
a reminder that the capsule was new, having been
installed a year earlier in compliance with safety
regulations. She almost smiled at the irony involved.
The old capsule had been equipped with full radio
communication and a Covell propulsion unit—either
of which could have been enough in her present
circumstance to make the difference between living
and dying.

*Brave new world! Another indication that humans had
turned their backs on space travel, that the dispersal of
whole cultures could be followed by pointing telescopes into
the night skies of the Big O's interior, charting the firefly
glows of their caravans and camps . . .*

As the minutes went by Jean's fear increased. A
normal reaction would have been to scan the band of
sky close to the Orbitsville horizon in the hope of
seeing marker lights drawing near, but she was unable to drag her gaze from the spurious depths below.
How far away was the shell now? Could the altime-

ter have been as haywire as everything else on the *Atkinson Grimshaw*, giving an inflated reading? Would the capsule's flashing beacons produce even the faintest smudge of reflection in the instant before the collision? Mesmerised, unblinking, Jean stared into the crawling darkness, trying to penetrate screens of after-images to reach the terrible reality beyond.

She had been that way for some time, her lips drawn into a unconscious grimace, when wonder intervened.

First appearing on the extreme left, a thin line of green radiance swept across the vastness of Orbitsville, moving so quickly from east to west that it crossed her entire field of view in less than a second.

Jean gave a sharp scream, keyed up to believe that any change in the unvarying blackness ahead signalled the final impact, then as quietness and stillness returned—as life continued—it began to dawn on her that she had witnessed the unthinkable. The fleeting green meridian had been a genuine phenomenon, an objective reality.

There had been a change in the enigmatic material of the Orbitsville shell.

Facing imminent death though she was, Jean felt a near-blasphemous excitement. Spherology was the name given to the science which had been born two centuries earlier when teams had first begun to study the shell material, and it was a discipline which was characterised by total lack of success. Even when viewed through a quark microscope the material appeared continuous—an embodiment of the pre-Democritus concept of matter—and in two-hundred years of concentrated effort no researcher had been able to make the slightest scratch on it or to alter it in any way. After millions of man-hours of study, spherologists knew the material's thickness, its albedo, its index of friction, and very little more.

It was, however, a basic tenet of their calling that the shell was immutable. And Jean Antony—swinging ever closer to it in the lonely darkness of her collision course—had seen a strange and transient stirring of life, like the first pulse of an embryo heart.

The attendant awe—for one who had spent half a lifetime flying that illusory black ocean—almost transcended the fear of death.

Chapter 6

In five weeks, with some medical assistance, Cona Dallen had learned to walk and to feed herself, and had almost completed her toilet training. According to Roy Picciano, senior physician for the community, her progress had been excellent—at least as good as would have been achieved had she been in full-time care at the Madison clinic. But as the sheer physical burden of looking after an adult-sized baby had gradually eased, the mental wear and tear on Garry Dallen had increased.

At first he had been too numbed by exhaustion and delayed shock even to consider Picciano's prognostication and advice. There had, for example, been no room in his mind for the monstrous suggestion that Cona might never again be able to speak. Her brain and nerve connections and muscles were all there, intact, and he—Garry Dallen, the man who never made a mistake—*knew* that by sheer perserverance and the force of his own will he would induce that delicate apparatus to function properly again.

The simple mind-filling truth which seemed to elude all doctors was that their science was based on studies of generalised humanity, on what had happened to anonymous masses of commonplace people, whereas in this case the subject was a unique and special entity who was central to Dallen's unique and special existence. Ordinary rules could not apply. Not this time.

The first unmanning blow had been the discovery that it was necessary for Cona and Mikel to live separately, because she was a real threat to the boy's safety. Cona is a baby again, had been the gist of Picciano's comments. She's locked in the true psychosis of the first weeks of infancy, unable to distinguish between herself and the outside world, with a feeling range which is limited to anger, pleasure, pain and fear. All babies react with violent anger when frustrated, especially where food is concerned. Given the necessary size and strength any infant would kill the mother who withdrew the teat too soon or who thwarted any other infantile desire. Cona is big and strong, particularly in comparison to Mikel, and one moment of rage is all it would take.

Dallen never failed to be dismayed each time that sudden fury asserted itself, usually over matters of diet. Cona had always had a strong appetite, and as a thinking adult had barely managed to control her weight by avoiding sweet and starchy foods. The new Cona, even after she had learned to chew, would have been content to subsist on nothing but chocolate and ice cream, and there were clashes when he tried to persuade her otherwise. Initially she had shown her anger by rolling on the floor and screaming, a sound which daunted him both with its volume and incoherence. At a later stage, when co-ordination and spatial awareness had developed, she had once succeeded in striking him on the face. The blow had stung, but the real pain had come in the swiftness of her transition from rage to crowing happiness as he had relaxed his grip on a disputed candy bar.

The message had been clear—*Cona Dallen doesn't live here anymore*—and it had caused him to back away, timorously, shaking his head in denial . . .

When Dallen answered the door chimes he was surprised to see Roy Picciano in place of the voluntary worker he had been expecting. It was mid-morning on a Tuesday and he had been planning some necessary shopping before going to the clinic to visit Mikel.

"Betti has been delayed for a while, so I offered to fill in for her," Picciano said, his smile showing the gold fillings which had again become fashionable. He was a bushy-haired, tanned man of about fifty whose preference for lightweight sports clothes created the impression that all his professional appointments were sandwiched between rounds of golf.

"Thanks, Roy." Dallen stepped back to let the doctor come in. "I could have waited, you know."

"It's no trouble. Besides, I wanted to have a look at my patients."

Dallen noticed the use of the plural. "I'm all right."

"You look tired, Garry." Picciano appraised him candidly. "How long are you going to go on like this?"

"As long as it takes. We've been through this before, haven't we?"

"No! *I* have been through it—you won't even begin to think about the problem."

"It's my problem. I'm responsible for Cona being the way she is."

"That's a perfect example of what I'm talking about," Picciano said, not hiding his exasperation. "You have no responsibilities to Cona, because Cona no longer exists. Your wife is *dead*, Garry. Your only responsibility now is to yourself. There is always some uncertainty about the progress of erasure cases, but there's one thing I can tell you for sure—the stunted, half-personality which is going to develop in that human shell in the next room will have nothing, *nothing* to do with your former wife. You've got to accept that, for your own good."

"For my own good." Dallen made the words sound like a phrase from a foreign language. "How long are we going to stand around here in the hall?"

"I'll look at her now." Picciano opened the nearest door and went into the long living room, his heels clacking on the polished composition floor. In his early attempts to deal with Cona's incontinence Dallen had tried putting her in diapers, but she had disliked them intensely, and he had found their appearance grotesque and degrading. He had then settled for removing all carpets and cleaning up after her, a chore which had almost ceased to exist now that she was using the bathroom. She was lying on a blue pneumat, chin propped on her hands, engrossed in watching the swirl of colours and shapes above a nursery imager. Her legs were bent, bare feet circling aimlessly and sometimes colliding. In spite of the loose smock in which Dallen had dressed her she was noticeably plumper than she had been a month earlier.

"Look who's come to see you," Dallen said, kneeling beside Cona and putting an arm around her shoulder. She glanced up at him, eyes bright with window reflections, and returned her attention to the glowing airborne patterns. Dallen took a tissue from his pocket and tried to dab a smear of chocolate from her chin, but she whimpered in irritation and twisted away from him.

"We only got the imager yesterday," Dallen explained. "It's still a novelty."

Picciano shook his head. "Do you know what you're doing, Garry? You're apologizing because the subject—I refuse to call her Cona, and so should you— didn't greet me with polite chitchat and a choice of coffee or sherry. This is what I've been . . ."

"For God's sake, *Roy!*"

"I'm only . . ." Picciano sighed and stared out of the window for a moment. "Did you get her to take all the fifth week medication and tracers?"

"Yes. No problem."

"In that case I'm going to carry out some tests and make notes." Picciano opened his flat plastic case and began to activate an instrument panel incorporated in the lid. "This is all routine stuff and I don't need any help," he added significantly.

"Thanks." Dallen pressed his face against Cona's for a moment without getting any response, then stood up and left the room. A minute later he was out on the street, breathing deeply to cleanse his lungs of the smell of chocolate and urine which in his fancy pervaded the house at all times. He lived near the outer edge of the inhabited strip of Madison, an area which straggled northwards for about five kilometres from the city centre to accommodate a population of several thousand Metagov and local administration workers. For the most part the dwell-

ings were large, stone-built and well screened by
trees—evidence of the district's former affluence. The
far-off drone of a lawnmower served only to empha-
sise the mid-week, mid-morning stillness, creating
the impression he had strayed into one of the thousands upon thousands of deserted suburbs which mi-
grating families had left to dreams and decay.

Windows and doorways, never aglow, Dallen thought,
recalling one of the most popular songs of the last
two centuries. *Everyone's gone to Big O . . .*

Dismissing the mawkish lyric, he decided to walk
into town and use the time to work on the problem of
Derek Beaumont. The tragedy that had befallen Cona
overshadowed everything else in his life, but he ap-
preciated a certain irony in the fact that the one man
he knew to bear responsibility also provided his only
distraction. When not grieving over his wife or cop-
ing with the despairing drudgery she now represented,
Dallen fantasised about being alone with the young
terrorist, about making him name all the relevant
names, about hunting and capturing and killing. Part
of him, even in lurid visions, drew the line at cold-
blooded execution, but another understood only too
well that confrontations could be manipulated. It was
a technique boys learned at school. Give the enemy a
gentle push, encourage him to push back, respond
with a harder shove, escalate the violence and keep
doing it until suddenly all thoughts of guilt can be
discarded and it's time to cut loose and go in hard.
When it's merely a matter of temperature, Dallen
knew, the blood can be very obliging. And the man
or woman who pulled the trigger on Cona and Mikel
was going to know the same thing . . . in the final
passionate, exultant moment that person was going to

know . . . and that person was going to be sorry . . .
in the end . . .

Walking south through slanting prisms of sunlight
and green shade, Dallen heard his own footfalls change
note as frustration hardened his muscles. Although
his job occasioned him to think and act like a
policeman, he held no official responsibility for local
law enforcement. He was a Grade IV officer in the
Deregistration Bureau, and as such his prime concern
was with surveying tracts of land that had been declared empty and making sure they remained unoccu-
pied for one full year, after which time Metagov was
longer legally accountable. Madison City itself, thanks
to the artificial mix of its population, had virtually no
crime, and the police department consisted of an
executive and a handful of officers who were mainly
concerned with regulating tourist accommodation. In
spite of the overlap in their jobs, Dallen had always
maintained an easy working relationship with Police
Chief Lashbrook. Consequently he had been surprised to find himself not only denied access to the
terrorist, but made distinctly unwelcome in the downtown police building.

"It was a sickening thing, what happened to your
wife and boy," Cole Lashbrook had said, eyeing him
severely over pedant's spectacles. "I'm deeply sorry
about it, but I've made every allowance I can. If you
persist with your attempts to see Beaumont I'll be
forced to take appropriate action against you."

Dallen's fists clenched as his sense of outrage
returned. "Against *me!*" he had almost shouted. "Are
you crazy?"

"No, but sometimes I think you are. Beaumont has
made a formal complaint about what you did to him

in back of that store, Garry. The dust hasn't settled over that business of the pursuit fatalities a couple of months back, and now there's this . . . And on top of it all you come round here and expect to be let loose on my prisoner!"

"*Your* prisoner?" Dallen had refrained with difficulty from pointing out the police department's past willingness to allow onerous duties to be performed by his own force.

"That's right. He was in possession of an explosive device and that makes it a criminal matter, and I intend to deliver Beaumont for trial in good health—a condition he may not be in if you get near him."

"Exactly what does that make me?"

"Garry, you're a man who has been known to go too far—even when you weren't personally involved in a case—and I'm not going to help you land yourself behind bars."

Thanks a lot, Dallen repeated to himself, immune to the blandishments of the placid sunlit warmth through which he was walking. In the two centuries since the discovery of Optima Thule, to give Orbitsville its constitutional name, there had been a general and steady decrease in traditional crime. Most crimes had involved property in one way or another, and as the race had been absorbed by a land area equivalent to five billion Earths—enough to support every intelligent creature in the galaxy—the basic motivations had faded away. Keeping pace with that change, many vast and complicated legal structures had become as obsolete as barbed wire, and progressively fallen into disuse.

Even on Earth, where there were historical complications, a community the size of Madison operated on a fairly informal basis as far as the law and its enforcement were concerned. In the days immediately following the blanking of his family Dallen had been certain that somehow he would obtain private interview with Beaumont. He had never allowed himself to consider the possibility of his being unable to force the prisoner to talk. He had fuelled himself night and day on the conviction that Beaumont would give him a name, *the* name, and that events thereafter would take a divinely ordained course. Now he was haunted by a suspicion that the young terrorist would be arraigned at the next session of the regional court and receive the routine sentence of—irony of ironies—deportation to Orbitsville. And once Beaumont reached Botany Bay, the popular name for the area surrounding the N5 portal, he would be beyond the reach of Dallen or any other private citizen. Economics and celestial mechanics had conspired to bring about that particular circumstance. A starship docking at an equatorial port simply went into orbit around Optima Thule's central sun, but only a few vessels—all owned by Metagov—were fitted with the complex grappling equipment which enabled them to cling like leeches to entrances in the northern and southern bands . . .

"What's wrong with your car, old son?" The voice from only a few paces away startled Dallen. He turned his head and found that a gold Rollac convertible had slowed to a crawl beside him without his noticing. The top was down and at the wheel was the buoyantly plump figure of Rick Renard, a man who had started showing up recently at the city gymnasium used by Dallen. Renard had red curly hair and milky skin which was uniformly dusted with freckles. He also had an uncanny ability to needle Dallen and

put him on the defensive with just about every remark he made.

"Why should anything be wrong with my car?"
Dallen said, deliberately giving the kind of response
Renard was seeking, as if to be wary of his snares
would be to pay the other man a compliment.

Renard's slightly prominent teeth gleamed briefly.
"Nobody walks in heat like this."

"I do."

"Trying to lose weight?"

"Yeah—right now I'm trying to get rid of about a
hundred kilos."

"I'm not *that* heavy, old son," Renard said, eyes
beaconing his satisfaction at having provoked an outright insult. "Look, Dallen, why don't you get in the
car with me and ride downtown in comfort with me
and use the time you save to enjoy a cold beer?"

"Well, if you put it like that . . ." Suddenly disen-
chanted with the prospect of walking, Dallen pointed
at the curb a short distance ahead, making the gesture
an instruction as to where to halt the car. Renard
overshot the mark by a calculated margin and scored
back against Dallen by allowing the vehicle to roll
forward before he was properly in, causing him to do
some quick footwork as the door closed.

"Aren't we having fun?" Renard's shoulders shook
as he enjoyed a private triumph. "What do you think
of the car?"

"Nice," Dallen said carelessly, slumping into the
receptive upholstery.

"This lady is sixty years old, you know. Indestructible. Brought her all the way fom the Big O. None
of your modern Unimot crap for me."

"You're a lucky man, Rick." Feeling the passenger

seat adapt itself to his body, coaxing him into
relaxation, Dallen was impressed by the car's sheer
silent-gliding luxury. It came to him that its owner
had to be wealthy. He vaguely recalled having heard
that Renard was a botanist who had come to Earth on
some kind of a field trip, which had suggested he was
a Metagov employee, but salaried workers did not
import their own cars across hundreds of light years.

"Lucky?" Renard's narrow dental arch shone again.
"The way I see it, the universe only gives me what I
deserve."

"Really? Do you accept donations from any other
source?"

Renard laughed delightedly. "As a matter of fact,
my mother was a Lindstrom."

"In that case, shouldn't the universe be getting
hand-outs from you?" Dallen closed his eyes for a
moment, glad to be distracted from his own affairs,
and considered Renard's claim to be related to the
legendary family which had once monopolised the
space travel industry. For a brief period after the Big
O's discovery its official designation had been Lind-
stromland, and the Scandinavian connotations of its
present name hinted at the clan's continuing if muted
influence. In their heyday the Lindstroms had amassed
a fortune which, apparently, was beyond human ca-
pability to diminish; and if Renard was connected
with them, no matter how tenuously, he was no
ordinary botanist.

The universe only gives me what I deserve. Dallen got a
mental image of his wife—wandering aimlessly through
shaded rooms, smock gathered to the waist, crooning
to herself as she masturbated on the move—and the

pressures within him grew intolerable. *Cona deserved better* . . .

"I heard you're a botanist," he said quickly. "You collect flowers?"

Renard shook his head. "Grass."

"Ordinary grass?"

"What's ordinary about grass?" Renard said, smiling in a way intended to let Dallen know that his education was incomplete. "So far we've found only thirty or so species on Orbitsville—an incredibly low number considering the areas involved and the fact that we have more than ten thousand species on Earth. The Department of Agriculture did some work on determining mixes of Earth seeds which are compatible with Orbitsville soil and the native species, but that was in the last century and it was a half-assed effort anyway. I'm doing the job properly. Soon I'll be going back with over a thousand seed varieties and maybe two thousand square metres of sample trays."

"So you work for Metagov."

"Don't be so naive, old son—all Metagov wants from Earth is a decree nisi." Renard turned the steering wheel with a languid hand, swinging the car into an avenue which ran due west. "I work for nobody but myself."

"But . . ." Dallen grappled with unfamiliar concepts. "The transport costs must be . . ."

"Astronomical? Yes, but it's not so bad when you have your own ship. For a while I considered chartering, then I realised it made more sense to recuse an old flickerwing from the graveyard and amortise the cost over three or four trips."

"That's what I would have done," Dallen said,

concealing his grudging awe for an indivdual who could so casually speak of owning the artificial microcosm that was a starship. "What have you got?"

"A Type 96B. It was designed for bulk cargo work, so there aren't any diaphragm decks, which means it isn't all that suitable for my work. But I got round that by building really tall racks to hold the grass trays. Do you want a free trip to Orbitsville?"

"No, not at . . . Why?"

"I need people to tend the samples by hand—not worth installing automatic systems—and I'm paying with free transportation. That way everybody benefits."

"Perhaps I'll become an entrepreneur."

"You're not cut out for it, old son—you've conditioned yourself to think *small*." Renard's smile conveyed affectionate contempt. "Otherwise you wouldn't be in the police."

"I'm not a policeman. I work for . . ." Dallen widened his eyes, belatedly aware of the car's change of direction. "Where the hell are we supposed to be going?"

Renard chuckled, again pleasurably triumphant in what appeared to be a never-ending personal game. "This will only take a couple of minutes. I promised Silvia I'd drop by with a carton of glass she's been waiting for."

"Silvia who?"

"Silvia London. Oh, I don't suppose you've ever been to the Londons' place?"

"Not since my polo stock got woodworm."

"I like you, Dallen," Renard said appreciatively "You are a refreshingly genuine person."

And you are a refreshingly genuine bag of puke, Dallen

thought, wondering how he could have been stupid enough to give up part of his day to such criminal waste. His previous encounters with Renard in the gymnasium had been brief, but they should have been enough to let him recognise and beware of a stunted personality. Renard's life appeared to be a continuous power game, one in which he never tired of contriving all the advantages, one in which no opponent was too small and no battlefield too insignificant.

The present situation, with Renard at the wheel of a car and therefore temporarily in control of his passenger's movements, was a microscopic annoyance, and yet the other man's obvious relish for what he was doing was turning it into something else. Furious with himself for being drawn in, Dallen nevertheless sat up straighter and began watching for an opportunity to quit the car. It would have to be done in a single effortless movement—otherwise Renard would score even more points—and for that the car would have to be practically at a standstill. Renard glanced sideways at Dallen and promptly accelerated, hastening the alternation of tree-shadow and sunlight over the curving gold hood.

"You'll enjoy meeting Silvia," he said. "You've got to see her jugs."

"Maybe I'm not interested in pottery."

"Maybe that's not what I mean, old son."

Dallen kept his gaze fixed on the pavement ahead. "I know what you meant, old son."

"I do believe he's angry!" Renard craned his neck to look into Dallen's face. "I do believe I've succeeded in provoking the puritanical Mr. Dallen. Well, well!" Shaking his head in amusement, Renard turned the car into a wide driveway with scarcely any slackening of speed. The level of illumination dropped abruptly as walls of foliage closed in on each side.

"These reactionary times we're living in must suit you very well." Renard spoke with quietly ruminative tones, surprising Dallen with the change of tack. "Personally, I'd have been happier thirty years ago, back in the Sixties. I suppose you've noticed the pattern in the last few centuries? The steady build-up of liberalism . . . peaking two-thirds of the way through . . . then the violent swing the other way to close out the century and start the next. Why do you think it happens? Why is it that Mary Poppins concepts like mortality and monogamy and family refuse to lie down and die?"

I'm going to presume he doesn't know what happened to Cona and Mikel, Dallen told himself. *When the car stops I'm going to walk way, and if he has enough sense to let me go that will be the end of it . . .*

The house which was coming into view on a low hill was not what Dallen had expected. All he knew about the Londons was that they were supposed to be wealthy and that they were a focal point for an unorthodox philosophical society—the sort of people whose chosen setting would abound in gabled roofs, leaded glass and all the overt signs of respectability and tradition. Instead, the London residence turned out to be a three-storey redbrick house—rather too small for its imposing location—around which had been tacked an untidy skirt of timber-framed extensions. Additions had been made to additions in an undisciplined manner which would not have been tolerated in the days when zoning regulations were taken seriously. A stack of greying lumber had been left near the entrance to the main building.

"Rebecca's replacement wouldn't have lost much sleep over this place," Renard said, bringing the car to a crunching halt on a square of brown gravel in front of the house.

Dallen nodded and remained silent, guessing that the allusion had been literary. He got out of the car and was turning to leave when a tall brunette in her late twenties came out to the front steps of the house to greet Renard. She was wearing a close-fitting white shirt and white pants which showed off a full-bosomed but lean-hipped figure. A hint of muscularity about her forearms suggested to Dallen that here was a woman who kept in trim by sheer expenditure of energy. Her face was small and quite square, with neat features and a slight prominence of chin which gave a near-truculent fullness to her lower lip. It was a face which in spite of its liveliness and intelligence, many would have considered disappointing, but Dallen found himself alerted and oddly disturbed, like one who is on the verge of recalling a vital missed appointment.

". . . and his name is Garry," Renard was saying to the woman. "I've never seen him go into a trance like this before—perhaps if you pointed your chest somewhere else . . ."

"Shut up, Rick. Hello, Garry." She gave Dallen a brief smile, her attention already focused on two transit cartons which rested on the rear seat of the car. "Is this my glass?"

"It certainly is, courtesy of Renard's doorstep delivery service. I'll carry it in for you."

"Thanks, but I'm quite capable of moving a box or

two." The woman reached into the car, picked up a carton and bore it away into the house.

"I'll say you are," Renard said admiringly, his gaze lingering on the white-clad figure before he turned to Dallen. "What did I tell you?"

Dallen felt a pang of annoyance then realised that what he disliked about the question was not so much the sexism as the proprietory pride. *This is crazy*, he thought, alarmed at the speed and uncontrollability of what was happening inside of him. *If a woman like that is mixed up with Renard she can't be a woman like that.* Unwilling to consider what his motives might be, he picked up the second carton and carried it into the house. Its weightiness confirmed his guess about Silvia London being physically strong. She met him at a doorway on the left of the hall, smiled again and gestured for him to go on through.

"Thanks," she said. "Straight ahead to the studio, please."

"Okey-dokey." *Brilliant conversational opening*, he thought, appalled. *Where did I dredge that one from?* He went through a high-ceilinged, conventionally furnished room and into another whose airiness and overhead windows proclaimed it to be part of the house extension. He came to a halt, transfixed, as he saw that the fierce light in the outer room was transformed into a multi-hued blaze by a screen of stained glass which reached almost to the ceiling.

Dallen's first impression was of a huge trefoil flower. All edges of the three enormous petals were in the same plane, which would have made it possible for the construction to serve as an incredibly ornate window, but the central surfaces were a bewildering series of complex three-dimensional curves, sculptures in glass. Geometric patterns based on circles and ellipses radiated from a sunburst centre, swirling and interacting, generating areas of intense complication in some places and smoothing into calm simplicity in others. The technique was almost pointillé, deriving its effect from myriad thousands of colour fragments, most of which were no bigger than coins. Dallen's sense of awe increased, rippling coolness down his spine, as he realised that the glowing tesserae—which he had taken to be brush-dabs of transparent paint—were actually individual chips of stained glass bonded with metal.

"My God," he said, with genuine reverence. "It's . . . I've never . . ."

Silvia London laughed as she took the carton from him and placed it on a nearby workbench. "You like it?"

"It has to be the most beautiful thing I've ever seen." Dallen filled his eyes with mingling rays, mesmerising himself. "But . . ."

"A third of a million."

"I'm sorry?"

"The first thing everybody asks is how many separate pieces of glass," Silvia said. "The answer is a third of a million, almost. I've been working on it continuously for four years."

"Why? For God's sake, *why?*" Renard spoke from behind Dallen, having entered the studio unnoticed. "With an imager you could have built up the same effect in a few days. Throw continuous computer variation and it would be even *better*. What do you say, Garry?"

"I'm not an artist."

"You could still venture an opinion." Silvia spoke

lightly, but her brown eyes were holding steady on Dallen's. "Why should I give up four years of my life to one unnecessary project?"

His answer was instinctive. "Something which sets itself up as a mosaic really has to *be* a mosaic—otherwise it's no use."

"Near enough," she said. "You can come back anytime."

"Crawler," Renard sneered. "Silvia, when are you going to drop this phoney reverence for old . . . what's his name . . . Tiffany and his methods? You know perfectly well that you cheat."

She shook her head, glancing at Dallen to include him in what she was saying. "I cut the glass with a valency knife because it's so fast and accurate. And instead of edging each piece with copper foil so that it can be soldered I transmute a couple of millimetres of it into copper, for reasons of speed and strength. But Tiffany himself would have used those methods if they'd been available to him—therefore in my book it isn't cheating."

"And how about the cold solder?"

"Same criterion applies."

"I should know better than to argue with a woman," Renard said, cheerfully unconvinced. "When are you and I going to have dinner?"

"We've been over all that."

Renard picked up a fish-shaped piece of streaky blue glass from the bench and peered through it. "How is Karal these days?"

"His condition is stable, thank you."

Renard held the strip of glass closer to his eyes, converting it into a mask. "I'm glad about that."

"Yes, Rick." Silvia turned to Dallen with an apologetic smile. "I'm sorry about the conversation becoming so cryptic. I'm not interested in adultery, you see—even though my husband is old and very ill. When I refused to date Rick a moment ago he, quite naturally—being the sort of person he is—asked me if Karal would die soon, and when I told him there was no immediate prospect of it he couldn't even make a convincing attempt to appear pleased."

"Silvia!" Renard looked scandalised. "You make me sound so *crass!*"

"I'm tempted to make the obvious reply to that one, but . . ."

"Don't mind me," Dallen put in. "I quite enjoy the sound of knuckles on flesh." He had slipped into his social armour by reflex, buying time in which to gain some control over what was happening behind his eyes. Information had been coming in too fast. The fantastic glass edifice filling the studio had an overpowering presence of its own, but something about Silvia London was even more disturbing. He had just learned that Renard had no claim on her, that she was a person upon whom Renard could not make a claim, and the result had been an immediate explosion of images and sense impressions—Silvia seen across a supper table; Silvia broodily examining a damaged fingernail; Silvia at the controls of a high-G zoom car; Silvia floating lazily in a sun-gilded pool; *Cona raising her gaze in momentary bafflement from an historical text*; Silvia lying with her head in the crook of his left arm; *Cona trailing footprints of her own urine from room to shaded room* . . .

Silvia looked thoughtfully at Dallen. "I can't help wondering . . . Have we met before?"

"It isn't likely," Renard said, grinning. "His polo stick got woodworm."

Dallen moved away from Silvia, closer to the stunning glass mosaic. "I thought this was a flower at first, but it's astronomical, isn't it?"

"Yes. It's a representation of a Gott-McPherson cosmos."

Dallen frowned, still expunging visions. "I thought McPherson was a spherologist. Isn't he on the Optima Thule Science Commission?"

"Yes, but it's his work on cosmogony that inspires me as an artist," Silvia said, caressing the glass with the tip of a finger. "Actually, as it stands the screen shows a pure Gott cosmos. The scenario he devised in the 20th Century called for the creation of three separate universes at the moment of the Big Bang. He labelled the universe we live in Region I. It's composed of normal matter and of course in our universe time goes forward. This is it in the left-hand zone, with all the colours and forms naturalistic by our terms of reference." Silvia crossed to the other side of the screen, stepping with care over a wooden support, choosing the constricted route between Dallen and the glass. Her hair touched his lips.

"In the opposite panel is the Region II universe, created in the same instant as ours, but rushing backwards into our past and composed of anti-matter. I've suggested its nature by using inverted forms and colours which are complements of those in Region I. Gott also postulated a Region III universe—a tachyon universe—which has sped far ahead of us in time and will remain in our future until all the universes meet each other again in the next Big Bang. This is the tachyon universe in the centre section—elongated abstract patterns, leached-out opalescent colours."

"Aren't you glad you asked?" Renard's bow of teeth gleamed. "If you want to appear intelligent and interested ask where McPherson comes into the picture."

"I'm sorry," Silvia said, her eyes again locking with Dallen's. "I do tend to presume that my private manias are universal."

"It's all right," Dallen replied quickly. "It's really . . . well, fascinating . . . and as a matter of fact I was going to ask about McPherson's contribution."

Renard burst into full-throated laughter, hamming up his scorn by slapping his thigh, and walked away into the old part of the house, shaking his head.

"Perhaps he's kind to animals," Silvia said, pausing until Renard was out of earshot. "McPherson refined Gott's ideas and also added a Region IV universe—an anti-tachyon universe which is fleeing ahead of Region II into its past. It's being incorporated into the design as a fourth panel complementing Region III, but there isn't enough ceiling height here to let me assemble the whole screen. That will have to wait."

"For what?"

"Completion of Karal's memorial college, of course."

"I see," Dallen floundered. "I'm afraid I don't know much about your husband's work."

"There's no real reason why you should—he isn't a publicity-seeker."

"I didn't mean . . ."

Silvia laughed, showing predictably healthy teeth. "You're far too normal to be keeping company with Red Rick, you know. Why do you do it?"

"He promised he could get me into movies," Dallen

said, trying to decide why he was unhappy about being described as normal. *What's going on here?* he thought. *I'm supposed to be the one who always holds the conversational high ground.*

"I'm sure you'd be interested in what Karal has to say." Silvia's gaze had a disconcerting softness. "We're having some people around tomorrow night—would you like to join us?"

"I . . ." Dallen looked down at the woman and felt a surge of genuine panic as he realised how close he had come to opening his arms to her. There had been no reason to it, no sense of having been given an invitation, not even any special pressure of desire—it was just that his arms had almost moved by themselves. *And Cona is still a prisoner, still where I put her.*

"I'm busy tomorrow," he said, his voice unexpectedly loud.

"Perhaps some other evening would . . ."

"My wife and I never go out." Dallen strode out of the studio and into the adjoining room, where he found Renard studying some botanical prints clustered on a wall. The high-ceilinged room seemed mellow and cool, part of another age.

"Ready to go?" Renard looked quizzical. "I thought an art lover like you would have been in there for ages. What have you been doing to this young man, Silvia?"

"Thanks for your help with the glass," she said to Dallen, entering the room behind him, and it seemed to him that her manner was now overly correct. "The cartons are quite heavy."

"No trouble. If you'll excuse me—I have an appointment in town." Dallen went out to the front of the house, prepared to leave the premises on foot, but

Renard caught up with him and within a minute—
after an exchange of formalities with Silvia—they
were in the car and rolling silently between banks of
foliage. Warm air currents touched Dallen's forehead.
The world looked subtley different to him, as in the
first moment after stepping out of a bar in daytime.
He felt that something momentous had happened,
but what made it unsettling was the lack of evidence
that anything at all had taken place. It was a matter
of interpretation. He had never met a woman quite
like Silvia London before, and could have been mis-
reading the signals because of unfamiliarity or male
egotism. Or perhaps sheer sexual deprivation. When
he had mentioned Cona's frequent masturbation to
Roy Picciano the doctor had suggested that it could
cease if they resumed a physical relationship, but
Dallen had found the idea repugnant beyond words . . .

"That was a nice little divertimento for all concerned," Renard said. "What went on in there?"

"Meaning?"

"The two of you came out of the studio like robots."
Renard looked amused. "Did you try to touch her?"

Dallen sighed in exasperation. "Stop the car and let
me out."

"No need to get huffy, old son," Renard said,
accelerating out into the street. "It's two years since
her old man went off to the Big O to die, and nobody
has got near our Silvia in all that time. It's a criminal
waste, really, but she has compensated by inventing
this game called New Morality Musical Beds. Cum-
bersome title, but I've just made it up. When the
music stops—by music I mean Karal's emphysematic
rattling—there's going to be one hell of a scramble,
and Silvia wants the field to be as large as possible.

I'm going to win, of course. It's a foregone conclusion, but she doesn't want to admit that to herself. I guess the illusion of choice gives her a bit of a lift."

The tone and content of what he had just heard outraged Dallen on behalf of Silvia, but he was distracted by new information. "I didn't realise Karal London lives on Orbitsville."

Renard nodded. "A place near Port Napier. He only appears in holomorph form at Silvia's little soirées, you know. Personally, I find it somewhat distasteful."

"A sensitive person like you would."

"Unkind, Garry, unkind."

"What's this about emphysema?"

"That's what is killing him. I'm told he can barely cross a room."

"But . . ." Dallen began to feel overwhelmed. *"Why?"*

"Why is he allowing himself to die of a disease which can be cured? Why didn't he either stay here or take Silvia to Big O with him?" Renard glanced at Dallen, arched teeth gleaming. "Obviously she didn't have enough time to get on to hobbyhorse number two otherwise you'd know all about it. That would have been something else for you to find . . . um . . . fascinating."

"Forget I asked," Dallen said, his patience fading.

"It's all part of the Great Experiment, man!" Renard laughed aloud, alerting the part of Dallen's mind that remained permanently on guard against being ribbed. "Haven't you heard you're going to live for ever?"

"I think somebody from Nazareth may have mentioned the idea."

"This is nothing to do with religion, old son," Renard said, apparently for once deciding to impart straight information. "Old Karal is anti-religious and anti-mystical. He set up his Anima Mundi Foundation a few years back with the express purpose of . . ."

"Garry? Have you got your ears on?" The voice came from Dallen's implanted transceiver. "This is Jim Mellor."

"I'm listening," Dallen sub-vocalised, shocked by the unexpected communication from his deputy after weeks of radio silence. "Is something wrong?"

"I've got some bad news for you," Mellor said. "Beaumont has escaped."

"Escaped!" Dallen felt old preoccupations take over his mind. "Pick him up again."

"It's too late for that," Mellor replied, sounding both angry and embarrassed. "It happened three days back, but Lashbrook only told me a few minutes ago. Beaumont will be back in Cordele by this time."

Dallen closed his eyes. "So I go to Cordele."

"What's the matter with you?" Renard said loudly from beside Dallen, an intruder from another dimension. "Are you talking to yourself?"

Dallen shut him out, concentrating on the exchange with his deputy. "Get a ship ready for me, Jim—I'll be with you in a few minutes."

"But . . ."

"In a few minutes, Jim." Dallen made the practised sideways movement of his jaw which switched off his transceiver, then tried to relax into the deep cushions of the seat. He felt a cold, pleasurable anticipation which—even though he could recognise it as a sickness—restored lost illusions of purpose.

Chapter 7

The Valley was not really a valley. It was a narrow strip, almost a kilometre in length, where Orbitsville's soil and bedrock had been scooped away to reveal a substantial area of shell material. Ylem was dark and non-reflective, so at night the strip had the appearance of a cold black lake. The research buildings anchored along it on suction foundations, continuously illuminated, looked like a flotilla of boats linked by power and communications cables.

Dan Cavendish had worked in the Valley for more than forty years, but he still got a contemplative pleasure from walking its length, knowing that only a few centimetres—the thickness of shell—beneath the soles of his boots was the edge of interstellar space. Since the death of his wife three years earlier he had found it difficult to sleep the night through, and had developed the habit of patrolling the strip from end to end in the darkness, meditating and remembering. Although devoid of stars, the Orbitsville night sky had a beauty of its own which was conducive to an old man's evaluation of his life.

The popular conception of the Big O was of a thin shell of ylem, 320 million kilometres in diameter, completely englobing a small sun, but scientists were very much aware of a second concentric sphere without which the entire system would not have been viable. It was much smaller than Orbitsville and non-material in nature, a globular filigree of force fields capable of blocking the sun's out-pourings of light and heat. It was composed of narrow strips, effectively opaque, whose function was to case great bars of shadow on the grasslands of Orbitsville, producing the alternating periods of light and darkness, day and night, necessary to the growth of vegetation. The inner sphere could not be studied directly, but its structure was observable in the bands of light and darkness moving across the far side of Orbitsville, roughly two astronomical units away. During a day period the banding showed as a delicate ribbed effect, barely noticeable, but at dusk the alternations of paler and deeper blue stood out vividly. And at night the hundreds of slim curving ribs became the dominant feature of the sky, swirling across it from two opposite points on the horizon, merging into a prismatic haze where they dipped behind denser levels of air.

Cavendish's life—all ninety-two years of it—had been spent on Orbitsville without his tiring of its beauty or its mystery. There were many questions about the incredible construct and he had refused to become dispirited over the fact that no answers had been forthcoming in spite of all the Optima Thule Science Commission's efforts. It was an article of his personal faith that a breakthrough was bound to come, eventually, and if possible he wanted to be on hand when it happened. That was why he was clinging to his job in defiance of all efforts to make him retire. Now that Ruth was gone his work was all that was left to him, and he had no intention of giving it up for anybody. In particular, he was not going to be squeezed out by Phil Vigus, the senior technical manager, with whom he had been conducting a private feud for several years. The intrusive thought of Vigus caused him to snort with anger.

"Thinks I'm over the hill, does he?" Cavendish said to the encompassing darkness at the eastern end of the Valley. "I'll show the schmuck who's over the hill."

He unfolded his portable stool and sat down to rest, dismissing from his mind the stray thought that talking aloud to himself could be evidence that Vigus's claims were justified. It was a fine night, with just a few wisps of cloud drawn across the striated sapphire of the sky, and he had the place to himself. All other staff members had gone to their bungalow homes and the absence of lights on the slopes surrounding the Valley showed they were in bed and asleep. Cavendish repressed a pang of envy and regret as he re-called the deep comfort of waking in the darkness and staying awake just long enough to touch Ruth's shoul-der and be reassured. They had had a good life together and he was not going to betray her at this stage by starting to feel sorry for himself. He took a deep breath, squared his shoulders and submerged his identity in the numinous magic of his surround-ings, the glowing enigma that was Optima Thule at night.

So many unanswered questions . . .

Who had built Orbitsville? And why? Was it really
an artifact, in the limited human sense of the word,
or was it—as some religious thinkers maintained—
evidence of a Creator who worked in diverse modes?
Could it be a manifestation of Nature in a form
which only seemed strange to men because of the
paucity of their experience?

As a native of Orbitsville, Cavendish was intinctively
inclined to the belief that it was a natural object, yet
he had always been perplexed by certain salient
features. There was, for example, the question of
gravity. By means which no man could begin to
understand, the thin shell of ylem generated gravity
on the sphere's inner surface—and none on the outer
surface—which suggested that Orbitsville had been
designed as a habitat. There was also the matter of the
portals. To a logical being there could be only one
explanation for the three bands of circular apertures.
They had to be entrances—but that led to the tricky
concept of God as Engineer.

Some could accept that idea easily; others objected
on the grounds that divine engineering should be
divinely perfect, whereas there were unaccountable
irregularities connected with the portals. Orbitsville
itself was exactly spherical, a symmetry to satisfy any
theologian, but why were there 207 portals on the
equator instead of some number more suggestive of
ethereal harmony? Why were the northern and southern bands not at precisely the same latitude, and why
were there 173 portals in the former and only 168 in
the latter? Furthermore, why did the portals themselves vary a little in size and spacing?

The arguments had been raging for two centuries,

with numerologists in particular mining their richest lode since the heyday of the Great Pyramid, but nothing was settled. Spherology continued with its record of non-achievement. Nobody understood why radio communications were impossible within the Big O. Nobody had analysed the mechanisms which kept the great shell in a stable relationship with the enclosed sun and its remote outer planet. Cavendish was an inorganic chemist and therefore was not professionally concerned with the problems of macrospherology, but on the personal level he had his yearning for an advance, even a single step forward, to be made in the time that was left to him. It would compensate for the forty-plus years of frustration he had experienced since coming to the Valley.

His lean frame balanced uneasily on the stool, Cavendish gazed along the line of buildings floating on their lake of ink. Some had been stripped down and rebuilt several times as series of experiments were terminated and others took their places. A number of the buildings and machines had inverted counterparts of themselves, like mirror images, clinging to the outside of the Orbitsville shell and positioned by dead reckoning from the edge of the nearest portal. Although separated from each other by a mere eight centimetres of ylem, no machine had ever been able to communicate with its opposite number. Cavendish was usually positive in his outlook, but there were times when he suspected that his field of endeavour, shell structure, was the least promising in the Commission's programme.

On a night like this, when the breeze was cool and it was difficult to remember his wife's voice, he could believe that more centuries would pass before ylem

yielded any of its secrets—and by then it might be
too late. Mankind would have dispersed into and
been absorbed by Orbitsville's infinite meadows. A
thousand times a thousand rural tribes would be permanently busy re-inventing the steam and internal
combustion engines, and would have no use for the
blueprints of the ultimate machine.

Cavendish gave a low sigh, deciding that he should
be in bed. He got to his feet and was stooping to pick
up the stool when the surface on which he was stand
ing blinked with green radiance. A line of light,
glowing on the full width of the Valley's floor, swept
by him, travelled the length of the strip and vanished
at its western end in a fraction of a second.

"What the . . . !" Cavendish stared into the familiar
backdrop of night, suddenly feeling unsafe.

He had lived all his life on the Orbitsville shell and
knew the material to be totally inert, changeless,
more stable by far than any planetary crust. It was
not supposed to pulse with green light . . . because if
that could happen other changes might occur . . . and
he could almost feel the ylem dissolving beneath his
feet . . . hurling his unprepared and unprotected body
downwards and outwards . . . into the space between
the stars . . .

Mark Denmark was obviously unhappy. He squared
up various stacks of paper on his desk, frowning all
the while, then went to the window of his office and
rocked on the balls of his feet while he inspected the
view. The Valley and its wide-eaved buildings and
the surrounding slopes reflected the sun's vertical
rays, looking exactly as they always did, embalmed in
brilliance which had an ancient Egyptian quality to

it. Denmark shook his head as though something outside had failed to pass muster, returned to his chair and began tapping his front teeth with a pen.

"Dan, we've *checked* every read-out from every instrument," he finally said. "There aren't any spikes. There aren't any blips or dips. In fact, there is simply no trace of any abnormal event."

"That's not surprising—considering we don't have any photometers aimed at the shell." Cavendish spoke in a matter-of-fact voice, concealing his disappointment over the lack of corroborative readings. He had been awake all night, voyaging on mental oceans of surmise, elated by the near-certainty that the science of spherology was about to take that long-awaited step forward. Now it was beginning to look as though he had taken a step backwards, lost ground in the battle over his delayed retirement.

Denmark leaned forward, hunching his shoulders. "Dan, I don't need to tell you that light can't come into being by itself. What you described sounded like an excitation phenomenon, but nothing got excited— except maybe your optic nerves."

"I'm perfectly healthy," Cavendish snapped. "Don't try that stuff on me."

"I'm only trying to stop you making a pig's ass of yourself. If you insist on your report going on log you'll draw a lot of attention, then you'll really find out what it's like to be under pressure. Christ, Dan, if everybody else can accept retirement at eighty, why can't you?"

"Because I'm not ready."

"Ready or not, one of these days . . . The Commission can insist, you know."

Cavendish glanced around the office in feigned

surprise. "Have I come to the wrong place? Are you the chief scientist or the personnel manager?"

Denmark's grey eyes clouded with annoyance and his mouth withered into a thin line. Watching the change of expression, Cavendish wondered if he had gone too far. Denmark was a natural researcher whose temperament had been poisoned by the constant struggle to keep all his projects functioning on dwindling budgets, and in the past months he had become moody and unpredictable. *All it takes is one word from him*, Cavendish thought, becoming alarmed. *Just one interoffice memo and I'm out in the cold with nothing but . . .*

"Good morning, men!"

The unexpected voice, coming from the open door, provided what Cavendish hoped would be a welcome diversion. He turned towards it and his spirits sank as he saw the stubby, bull-necked form of his old adversary, technical manager Phil Vigus, entering the office. Vigus, who was ultimately responsible for the reliability of all equipment, took every complaint as a personal insult—a trait which had often brought him into conflict with Cavendish. He had long regarded Cavendish as a cantankerous geriatric, and at that particular moment was the last person Cavendish wanted to see.

"Take a seat, Phil," Denmark said. "I'm glad you dropped by."

"Really?" Vigus lowered his bulk into a chair. "What have I got that you want?"

Denmark gave him a cold fleeting smile. "You've got millions of monits' worth of equipment strung out along the Valley, and I've just been informed by Mr. Cavendish here—who else?—that it's a load of crap. I used to think the shell material was inert, didn't you? Well, apparently ylem can become so agitated that it lights up like a traffic sign, and not one of your piss-poor instruments even gives a quiver. What do you think of that?"

"That's not what I said," Cavendish protested, shocked by the sheer crudity of Denmark's attack and deducing from it that he had landed himself in a genuine crisis. This was a tailor-made chance for Vigus to come down on him with both feet, to add his managerial clout to that of Denmark. Both men working in unison could have him issued with his walking papers in a couple of hours.

"I presume, from the scuttlebut I picked up this morning, that we're talking about Dan's wonderful green flash." Vigus's lips twitched in amusement. "They're already calling it his nocturnal emission."

"That's it," Denmark said gleefully, and having been presented with a joke went on, as humourless people do, to run it ragged. "Some people get hot flushes at night—Dan gets green flashes. What do you say, doc? Is it a serious ailment?"

"I can tell you one thing about it." Vigus stared hard at Cavendish for a second, eyes unreadable, his expression curiously benign.

Executioner's compassion, Cavendish thought. *Here comes the big knife.*

"Tell me the worst," Denmark prompted.

"It's infectious," Vigus said. His tone was calm, very neutral, but Cavendish felt a premonition.

Denmark looked disappointed. "What does that mean?"

"I read a lot of reliability reports, from all over. Not just on research equipment, on nearly anything.

Three weeks or so ago a pilot called Jean Antony baled out of an old freighter on the equatorial run, close to 156. The ship apparently was a deathtrap, *nothing* working right, and she got herself ejected downwards. Her capsule actually grazed the shell before it was recovered, so it was a near-miracle she got out of it alive." Vigus paused for an unnecessarily long time, still looking at Cavendish.

"Stirring stuff," Denmark said drily, "but I don't . . ."

"Just before the collision Jean Antony saw a green flash. Just like Dan's. She described it in her accident report, but nobody paid any heed. It was written off as nerves or a stray reflection on the capsule's transparencies."

Denmark nodded. "I'd say nerves—you know what women are like."

"This one saw a thin band of green radiance moving fast across the shell from east to west," Vigus asserted. "Something is happening, Mark—something very unusual—and the sooner you report Dan's observations to Commission HQ the more credit you'll be able to grab for yourself."

"I'd like to thank you," Cavendish said to Vigus as they left the admin building together. "If you hadn't chimed in when you did . . . Mark was all set to dump me, you know."

"He'd only have been forced to take you back on again, after you'd become famous." Vigus grinned in the vertical prism of shadow cast by his coolie-style hat. "You're going to be insufferable enough as it is."

"Thanks a lot," Cavendish said, pretending to be insulted, but feeling better inside than he had done at any time in the three years since his wife had died. Life, it would seem, still had something to offer.

Chapter 8

Dallen took the little patrol ship to a height of eight thousand metres—enough to render it invisible from the ground—and drifted in over Cordele from the north. About a third of the built-up area had been destroyed by old fires, but from the air large tracts looked almost as they would have done forty years earlier when the city was being officially deregistered. Only the high proportion of greenery, obliterating the street patterns in some places, hinted at the progressive decay which would eventually erase all obvious signs of habitation. Armies of wood-boring insects were hard at work down there, tidying up the stage for the benefit of future performers.

The map projected on the navigation screen beside Dallen was decades out of date—in the eyes of the Metagov cartographers Cordele no longer existed—but it was adequate for his purpose. He touched a button which activated the ship's scanning system and a bright red dot appeared in the middle of a western suburb. It was standard procedure with the Madison police to radio tag some personal item belonging to detainees, often a belt buckle, and now the coded signal was telling Dallen exactly where he would find the man he was hunting.

He watched the glowing speck long enough to assure himself it was not moving, then swung the ship into a curving path which took it out across the blurry-edged strip of solder which was the Flint River. Twenty kilometres west of the city Dallen made a rapid descent through the heavy water-logged air, watching the atlas-page sweep of territory below him expand to become a sunlit reality clothed with vegetation which moved visibly with changes in the wind. At a height of only a few metres he skimmed eastwards, taking advantage of every irregularity in the terrain to hide his approach to the city. The outer ring of abandoned restaurants, motels and commercial buildings appeared ahead of him, many of the structures completely obscured by kudzu vines. Dallen threaded the ship through them in silence, bringing it as close to his destination as he dared, and grounded by the sheared-off side of a small hill.

He studied the map display for a moment, noting that he was some three kilometres from his target, then took off a print which he folded and put away in his pocket. He was confident that he could go straight to Beaumont without extra guidance, but returning to the ship might not be so simple and he wanted to minimise the risk of getting lost. After checking various pieces of equipment, including his sidearm and quarry finder, he slid the pilot door open and stepped down onto a thick carpet of moss and ground-hugging creepers. Going by the book, he should have retracted the slim tubes of its wing field generators before leaving the ship unattended, but in the interests of a quick getaway he chose not to do so. Nobody was likely to chance upon the ship and in any case the tubes, which were the only vulnerable part, had been freshly coated with repellant paint.

It was a little past noon and a thickly murmurous heat lay over the surroundings, the main elements of which were overgrown shrubs and ruinous single-storey houses. A plastic-skinned microbus stood nearby, contriving to look almost serviceable after more than forty years, except for the tree which had grown up through the engine compartment.

Dallen set off in the direction of the city centre, walking quickly, checking his progress with those street signs which were still legible. The tension that was growing within him manifested itself in his increasing jumpiness. He fought it by refusing to think about what lay ahead, absorbing images of his environment, turning himself into a camera. Concrete light poles had crumbled here and there, doubling over and exposing ferrous brown veins. Some houses which had looked quite intact from a distance were revealed as mere clay overlays erected by termites, the enclosed timbers long since digested. On the window of a store, miraculously still intact, some long-departed humourist had sprayed the words, GONE TO LAUNCH.

Dallen experienced a growing sense of bafflement. Why did people cling on in places like this? He knew there were parts of the world where human labour had again become valuable, where the petty chieftains of the new age—men who could feel their power growing as Orbitsville lost interest in Earth—prevented their slave-subjects from taking the big trip. But it

had always been different on the NorAm continent—so
why had a few chosen to remain behind in conditions
like this? Question to be taken literally: what on
Earth possessed them? Dallen cursed as the words of
the old song, the one he had always disliked, paraded
behind his eyes . . .

Streets fallen silent, blowing dust,
Railways and bridges, growing rust,
Christmas is only untrodden snow,
Everyone's gone to Big O . . .

The sounds of children at play startled him into
alertness. He paused and listened to the faint but
unmistakable pleasure cries which might have been
drifting through a time warp from a previous century.
There were seven blocks between him and his target,
but he deduced he was reaching the edge of an enclave which possibly was guarded. He moved forward with greater caution, one hand gripping the
sidearm concealed in his pocket, and reached an intersection where the pavement had been lifted and frag-
mented by trees and their roots. A stand of rank
grass and weeds provided cover from which he was
able to reconnoitre the street ahead.

Vegetation was much in evidence everywhere, ob-
scuring the signs of habitation, but he saw at once
that the houses had been deliberately thinned out and
that the empty spaces were under cultivation. Although no people were directly visible, he could see a
vehicle moving in the distance and from somewhere
nearby there came the bleating of a sheep. Sensing
that it would be pointless to try moving through such
an area undetected, Dallen left the shade of the trees
and walked openly along the street, his stride casual
but long. A group of small children, shabbily dressed

but healthy looking, came running out of nowhere
chanting a play rhyme and as quickly disappeared
behind hedges.

Their presence was somehow disturbing to Dallen,
then he realised he had always unconsciously thought
of the Independent communities as being entirely
composed of mulish disgrunted adults. *Over-simplifica-
tion*, he thought. *An occupational disease of Deregistration
Bureau workers.*

Cordele had been depopulated in 2251 and kept
empty for the statutory whole year, which meant
that the people now living in it did not exist as far as
Metagov was concerned. The convenient administrative fiction was that none of the small groups of
dissidents who wandered in the spreading wilderness
of the country would have been attracted to the deserted cities. But shelter and other necessities were to
be had for the taking there, and the cities could again
serve in their most basic role—places where those
who needed to could band together for mutual support.
In those circumstances children were bound to arrive,
officially non-existent children, disenfranchised, not
entitled to education or even the most rudimentary
health care.

I'm getting out of the Bureau, Dallen told himself
once again. *As soon as I collect my back pay—as soon as I
get what I'm owed for Cona and Mikel.*

He made steady progress towards his destination,
encountering more and more people as he got farther
into the enclave. Some of the adults eyed him curiously as he passed, but showed no inclination to
challenge him. Either the local population was large
enough for a stranger to remain inconspicuous, or the
people were less defensive and insular than he had

supposed. At a corner of one block he saw an open-air produce market apparently running on the barter system, and the presence of several mud-spattered trucks indicated that somebody was farming on a comparatively large scale.

On reaching the seventh block inwards Dallen found that it was non-residential, the side he was nearest being occupied by a brick-built church, a bank and a three-storey hotel. The hotel was the only building of the three which looked as though it had been kept in use. Making sure he was not being watched, Dallen took out the quarry finder—which was tuned to the signal from Beaumont's belt buckle—and looked at its circular screen. A crimson arrow glowed on its surface, pulsing rapidly, pointing to the hotel. Aware of the measured thudding of his heart, Dallen angled across the street. He entered the off-street parking area and had almost reached the building's entrance when a thick-set man materialised in the dense shade of the canopy. The man was youngish, prematurely grey, and had a pump-action shotgun slung on his shoulder.

"Where do you think you're goin', fella?" he said, sounding curious rather than hostile.

Dallen absorbed the fact that the hotel was serving as some kind of headquarters. "I've got to see the boss."

The man extended a hand, husking thumb and fingers together. "Papers."

"Sure thing." Dallen smiled, slipped his hand into his jacket pocket and fired the sidearm without taking time to grip its handle. The wide-angle cone of radiation sleeted through the guard's body, turning him into an organic statue. Dallen closed with him before he could topple and, taking a chance on the small lobby being empty, waltzed the rigid form back into the hotel. A door beside the desk looked as though it led to staff washrooms. It was necessary to take another risk, but Dallen had begun to feel supercharged with confidence, like a man high on felicitin, and he bore the guard through the door without pause. The room beyond was empty. It took him only a few seconds to bundle the inert figure into a closet, then he was out in the lobby and running for the stairs.

On the second-floor landing he checked with the quarry finder and got a reading which told him to go left. Dallen hurried silently along the corridor, dragging the sidearm from his pocket, and halted at a door which was indicated by an abrupt swing of the bright arrow. Allowing no time for reflection, filled with a heady certitude, he twisted the handle and went through the door fast. The room contained one bed upon which was lying a black-haired woman of about twenty, naked except for a rumpled waist slip. She stared up at Dallen without moving. Items of her discarded clothing were draped on a chair, among them a durocord skirt and a man's belt with a metal buckle.

"It's Beaumont I want," Dallen said in a fierce whisper, unable to accept that something had gone disastrously wrong. "You'll be all right as long as you keep quiet. Do you understand that?"

The woman nodded, opened her mouth and screamed.

"You stupid . . !" Dallen almost silenced her with his paralyser, then realised there would be no point. The scream seemed to have been amplified rather than damped by the building's partition walls and he could already hear startled male voices in an adjoining room. He turned back to the door, thoughts in turmoil, and was trying to choose between two unpromising courses—running for the street or locking himself in—when the woman pulled the trigger.

Harry Sanko, "mayor" of West Cordele, was wearing a full business suit, complete with traditional-style collar and tie, regardless of the moist heat. He was in his early forties and had regular features with a Latin cast which was emphasised by a neat pencil-line moustache. He was well-fed, articulate, forceful in his manner and smiled a lot in spite of having only one front tooth.

"What you did was stupid," he said to Dallen. "The only word for it is . . . well . . . *stupid*."

Dallen managed to nod in agreement. He had been dragged the length of the corridor to a conference room and had been pushed into one of the high-backed chairs which surrounded a circular table. Sanko was sitting opposite him and two burly young men armed with shotguns were standing at the door. The fact that Dallen was able to move his head meant that he had been zapped with a low-power personal defence weapon, but he derived scant comfort from the knowledge. He was very much aware of being totally helpless.

"Marion is a close friend of mine," Sanko went on. "She's a protégée, you might say . . . and if you had touched her . . . or if you had used this on her . . ." He tapped Dallen's sidearm, which was lying on the table in front of him, and shook his head, apparently awed by inner visions of his retribution.

"I told you I was only interested in Beaumont,"

Dallen replied. "I didn't know your so-called protegée had his belt."

Sanko leaned forward and showed his single tooth. "You are quite a stern character, aren't you, Dallen? You're sitting there, paralysed, helpless, not knowing whether I'm going to have you strung up or castrated with a blunt knife, yet you can't help referring to Marion as my *so-called* protegée. A man in your shoes should be more diplomatic. I mean, how do you know I'm not sensitive?"

"People who plant bombs usually aren't."

"So that's it!" Sanko stood up, walked quickly around the table and sat down again, hard enough to make his chair creak. "I've got news for you, Mister Metagov—this is a civilised community here in West Cordele. We've got laws, and we enforce them. We don't have electricity or clean water or any amenities like that, but we're not savages. We don't go in for terrorism."

"Beaumont does."

"Beaumont was a brainless punk."

"*Was?*" Dallen's fingers twitched, first sign of returning mobility. "Does that mean . . . ?"

"It means he's dead. He was tried and executed yesterday along with two of his buddies—for stealing community property. Does that seem a trifle harsh to you?"

"No—just barbaric."

Sanko gave a barely visible shrug. "You've got to understand that in any Independent community almost the worst crime anybody can commit is the crime of waste. We have a small cash reserve for buying black market medical supplies, and Beaumont and his brother cretins blew some of it on bomb kits.

A few months back two of them wrecked one of our last working automobiles, and if they hadn't totalled themselves along with it we'd have had to . . ." Sanko broke off and gazed solemnly at Dallen, his tooth digging into his lower lip.

"I don't get this," he finally said. "Why are you here? What was Beaumont in your soft little life?"

"The day I pinched him in Madison he said his friends were going after my family." Dallen spoke slowly and carefully, his mind laboring to assimilate the news of Beaumont's death and the wider implications of what he had just heard. "About the time he was saying that somebody went into the City Hall and used a Luddite Special on my wife and son . . . but . . ."

"But what, Mister Metagov? Brain beginning to stir? How much cash does it take to buy one of those fancy toys?"

A corrosive acid was seeping through Dallen's mind, burning away one world-picture, disclosing another. "Somebody in Madison . . . Probably somebody in City Hall itself . . ."

"What were you saying about barbarism a minute ago?"

"But I can't see why," Dallen went on. "There was no reason for it."

"Maybe a slug of this will get your head working." Sanko took a silver flask from his pocket, came round the table and poured some of its contents into Dallen's mouth. "A Luddite Special is its own reason, man. It only does one job."

"There can't . . ." Dallen gagged as warm neat liquor reached his throat, but the spasms seemed to accelerate the return of sensation to his limbs. He became aware of a twitching in his calf muscles.

"Your wife and kid must have known something. They must have seen something." Sanko drained the flask and tossed it to one of the armed men who caught it and left the room unbidden. "You're no Sherlock Holmes, are you?"

Dallen wasted no time in speculating who Sherlock Holmes was. He was appalled at his own lack of perception, at the weeks he had wasted, at his unconscious arrogance in assuming that he and his futile, insignificant, Earth-limited activities had been the root cause for what had happened to Cona and Mikel. The alternative theory was that there was a monster roaming loose in Madison City, enjoying the immunity that Dallen had personally gifted to it—but what had been the original crime? What could have been sufficiently serious to justify the erasure of two personalities? Had it been a murder? The circumstances did not fit—nobody had been found dead or reported missing.

"It still doesn't make sense," Dallen said. "We don't have any serious crime in Madison."

"I love it!" Sanko laughed aloud, his mouth and the solitary tooth forming a notched dark circle. "Graft doesn't bother anybody in Madison and that means it isn't serious."

"There might be some petty . . ."

"Listen to me—Madison City is a kind of general store for all the big Independent communities in this part of the world. They come from as far away as Savannah and Jacksonville, any place that can scrape up big money, and it's from Madison they buy their generators, water purifers, truck engines, whatever. Didn't you know?"

"I know my wife and son weren't involved."

"You're starting to bore me, Dallen. How did you get to Cordele? By car?"

"I flew."

"That's a pity—if you'd come by car we'd have taken it and let you walk back. A flier is no use to us though, so I guess you can take it away as soon as you've thawed out."

It was only then that Dallen realised he had been expecting imprisonment or worse. "You're letting me go?"

Sanko looked exasperated. "Maybe you expected to be cooked and eaten."

"No, but with what I know about Beaumont . . ." Dallen paused, deciding not to make a case for his detention.

"Try a little experiment," Sanko said, taking Dallen's sidearm and dropping it into his own pocket. "When you get back to Madison make out a report saying you heard some non-existent people claiming to have ended the non-existence of some other non-existent people. I'd like to hear what sort of reaction you get."

It was late afternoon when Dallen reached the city. He circled in low over the south-western districts, over Scottish Hill and the immaculate, hermetically sealed suburbs which would later begin to glow in a simulation of life as the lights came on in a thousand empty streets. The tall buildings of the city centre, projecting above vivid toyland greenery, were washed with sunlight and looked impossibly clean, idyllic. A visitor winging down from space might have concluded that here was a community of contented, rational beings leading well-regulated lives—but Dallen's mood was one of disaffection as he picked out the pastel geometries of the City Hall.

His reckless dash to Cordele had, as well as providing vital information, jolted him out of grief-dominated patterns of behaviour, freed him from the emotional conviction that a craving for justice and revenge would, if strongly enough felt, bring about its own ends. He had been reminded that there was no even-handed arbiter, and that the most successful hunters were those who stalked their prey with coldness and calculation.

His ship hovered for a moment, then began its purposeful descent, its shadow a drifting prismatic blur which advanced and retreated according to the lie of the land beneath.

Chapter 9

Gerald Mathieu stood at the window of his office and watched the Bureau patrol ship slant down across the sky for a landing at Madison's inner field. The notion that Garry Dallen might be at the flying controls entered his mind, but he dismissed it and walked back to his desk. Dallen's prolonged absence from the City Hall had been welcome to Mathieu as a breathing space, but it was making him obsessive, giving his subconscious mind too much time to elaborate on the image of a dark superhuman Nemesis.

He had survived his encounter with Dallen immediately after the incident . . . *woman and child, crumpling, falling, idiot eyes shining* . . . but the circumstances had been exceptional and had not quite dispelled his fear of the other man's intuitive power. Since then that fear had been growing, week by week, and now the prospect of eventually having to face Dallen again ranked with all the other great phobias of his life. There was the dread of venturing into infinite black space, of living in a wafer-thin shell of alien metal, of being exposed as a criminal, of ever having—even once—to exist for a full day without felicitin. And now there was the next meeting with Garry Dallen . . .

Mathieu sat down at his desk and tried to concentrate on the backlog of work. The job of mayor or deputy in an artiticial city bore little resemblance to that traditionally associated with the titles. It was more akin to being executive officer for a very large theme park, and Mathieu's responsibilities ranged from public relations and tourist information to recruitment and purchasing. Even with extensive electronic assistance the job was demanding, especially as the city's annual revenue was in a steady decline. Mathieu had deferred for several days decisions about reducing engineering budgets, but on his way to the office that morning had promised himself good progress. It would be a sign that he was still functioning well, that a single unlucky accident . . . *woman and child, crumpling, going down before him, minds blown away* . . . was not going to ruin his entire career.

He called up a set of cost analysis graphs on the desk's main screen and strove to link the varicoloured blocks and lines to external reality. Silent minutes went by. The graphs shimmered on the surface of his eyes, tantalising him by refusing to be drawn into his head. He was beginning to feel a mild panic when the internal communicator chimed and Mayor Bryceland's features appeared at the projection focus, eyes blindly questing. Taking only a second to smooth down his jacket, Mathieu accepted the call, making himself visible at the caller's terminal.

"Let's have a talk about the conference," Bryceland

said at once. "What have you got so far in the way of a programme?"

Mathieu was baffled for a moment, then it dawned on him that Bryceland was referring to a conference of museum city managers which Madison was scheduled to host in the coming November. "I haven't had a chance to look at it yet, Frank," he said. "Perhaps next week . . ."

"Next week!" Bryceland's puffy countenace registered dismay. "I suppose you're aware how important this conference is?"

"Yes. I'm also aware it's five months away."

"Five months is no time at all," Bryceland grumbled. "Specially the way you're working these days."

"Meaning?"

"Try to figure it out for yourself." Bryceland's image dissolved into transient specks of light, ending the conversation.

"Jesus *Christ!*" Mathieu leaped to his feet, fists clenched, angry and afraid at the same time. He walked around the office and paused at his full-length mirror for reassurance. The blond-haired figure gazing at him from the safety of that *other* office, the one in the looking-glass world, appeared exactly as it should—tall, young, athletic, successful, immaculate. But were the eyes beginning to show signs of strain? Was there a slight hunching of the shoulders which indicated harmful tensions?

Mathieu raised one hand to touch the rose-petal perfection of his white collar, but the figure in the mirror betrayed him. It guided the hand to the inner pocket of his jacket, and found himself holding the gold pen, the one which dispensed a magical ink. He hesitated, trembling on the edge. It was regarded as medically impossible for anyone to kick the felicitin habit unaided, but since the day of the incident . . . *woman and child, crumpling, unique human flames guttering* . . . he had been holding off on the fixes until after office hours. The motive had been self-defence, the plan to avoid dangerous confidence, but five weeks had gone by and his position had to be growing more secure with each passing hour. And there might be a greater hazard in the displaying of personality changes dating back to the precise day of the crime . . . *woman and child, crumpling, falling* . . .

He clicked the pen's changeover mechanism and quickly drew the point across his tongue.

As he was returning the gold cylinder to his pocket he felt a twinge of curiosity about the exact amount of felicitin left in its reservoir. There was no anxiety involved, no urgency, simply a mild desire to confirm that all was well. He raised the pen to his eye and rotated it until the light from the window was caught in an integral glass capillary. The shock was almost physical, dragging his mouth out of shape, causing him to take a step backwards.

There was under a week's supply, where there should have been enough for a month.

Along with the confirmation that he had been using too much of the drug came the first surge of induced reassurance, blessed certainty that he could handle any difficult situation which arose. Felicitin, as he had noted before, worked fast.

The main problem to be considered was that his supplier was not due in from the west coast for another two weeks, and the solution was straightforward—he would cook up a good reason and make a special flight to Los Angeles. QED. Everything would be fine. In fact, now that he thought about it constructively, discovering that his drug stock was low was one of the best things that had ever happened to him. The pen dispenser was a rich man's toy—making it far too easy to take an over-generous dose—so from next week onwards he was going to use microcaps. That system was much better. It would give him a foolproof method of monitoring his consumption, would also save him a lot of money, and would also be a major step towards the day when he would be able to quit using the drug altogether.

All was well with his world—and the wondrously heartening aspect of it was that things could only get better . . .

Mathieu adjusted the hang of his jacket to his satisfaction, smiled at his reflection in the mirror, and sauntered back to his desk.

Chapter 10

Dallen had endured the emptiness and quietness of the house for as long as his temperament would allow, and now he had begun to get a last-man-in-the-world feeling.

From the front window he could see most of one shallow slope of the city's North Hill, and there was no sign of movement anywhere in that expanse of nostalgic blue dusk. The progressive appearance of lights—distant speckles of gold, peach and amber—provided little comfort, because he knew that automatic switches were producing exactly the same effect in the uninhabited districts of Limousin, Scottish Hill and Gibson Park. Everything looked right for the tourists gliding down from orbit on the evening shuttle, but from where Dallen stood it was almost possible to believe that Earth's last citizens had been spirited away while he was dozing.

The words of the old song tried to invade his mind . . . *Out on the freeway, moonflowers blow; Everyone's gone to Big O* . . . but he blocked them off, turning away from the window to walk through silent rooms in which his imagination still detected a hint of urine. Yesterday there had been a message from Roy Picciano explaining that he had, in view of Dallen's late return, taken Cona to the clinic for extra tests which would last at least three days. Give yourself a break, the recording had concluded, take a couple of days off.

At first Dallen had been unable to accept the advice. The sortie to Cordele had left him physically tired, but he had driven to the clinic and spent time with Cona and Mikel. She had been bored and then angered by his attempts to get her to speak, and the boy had been asleep in his cot in the adjoining room, one hand clutching a tiny yellow truck. Dallen sought consolation in the fact that Mikel still had a special liking for toy vehicles, but it was a desperately thin lifeline. The infant personality had been erased before it had properly formed—so how could it ever be retrieved? You want a replacement for your baby son, sir? Must have a fondness for miniature cars? Wait just a moment, sir—we've got the exact model you need . . .

Dallen had left the clinic with a tearing pain in his throat and a dark chill gathering in his mind. He could go to the chief of police with a new theory about the five-week-old crime, but Lashbrook would seize on the lack of obvious motive as an excuse to take no action. In any case, Dallen reminded himself, he had no wish for the culprit to be taken by the authorities and shipped off to Botany Bay. The punishment would have to be much more drastic, personally administered, a venting of suppurative poison, and for that he would have to find the guilty person unaided.

And there still remained the enigma of the motive. Glib words about a Luddite Special being its own motive explained everything and nothing. What he needed was a credible reason for somebody who worked in City Hall to use such a device on an innocent woman and child, and his brain seemed quite unequal to the task. Grief, bitterness and undirected hatred were no aids to analytical thought.

It was in that state of mind that Dallen had fallen asleep in an armchair after reaching home. When he had wakened in the middle of the night there had seemed no point in transferring to a lonely bed, so he had stayed in the chair till morning. A full day spent in brooding, snacking and dozing had further reduced his drive, and now he felt too dispirited to think at all. The house had become a tomb, a prison, a place from which he had to escape. Ceasing his aimless drifting, he took a cool shower, shaved and changed into fresh clothing, all the while telling himself that he had no definite plans, that he might be going to the gymnasium or to a bar or to his office. It was not until he had actually started the engine of his car and had to choose a destination that he acknowledged he was going to see Silvia London.

He drove south with the top down, following the route he had traversed the previous day with Rick Renard. A few major stars were visible through the city's canopy of diffused light, forming a sparse background to Polar Band One, which was nearing zenity. The north-south line of space stations and parked ships had once been a brilliant spectacle in the night sky, but it had dimmed as the era of the great migrations had drawn to a close. Now it was mainly composed of irreparable hulks, many of which had been partially cannibalised to enable other ships to make final departures for Orbitsville. Dallen could only see it as a symbol of Earth's decline and he had no regrets when turning west removed the thinly jewelled braid from his field of view.

Lights were on all over the London residence and its extensions, and the presence of at least twenty cars on the apron of gravel added to the impression that there was a sizable party going on inside. Dallen, who had been expecting a much smaller gathering, swung his car into a vacant space and got out, discovering that he was close to Renard's gold Rollac. He hesitated for a second, suddenly dubious about entering the house, then noticed Silvia at a ground-floor window in animated conversation with someone he could not see. The vertical rays from an overhead lamp emphasised the pouting fullness of her lower lip and highlighted her breasts, making her look impossibly voluptuous, like a sexist illustration on a cassette cover. He watched her for a moment, feeling like a voyeur, and went into the house.

"Welcome to this informal meeting of Anima Mundi Foundation!" The voice came from a thin, high-shouldered man of about sixty who was standing in the centre of the square hall. He was casually dressed in slacks and floral shirt, but his silver-bearded face had a conscious dignity which would have been more in keeping with donnish robes. A bar of unnaturally high colour reached from cheekbone to cheekbone across the saddle of his nose.

"Is this your first visit to one of our discussion evenings?" he said, giving Dallen a formal smile.

"Yes, but I only came to . . ." Dallen broke off as he realised he was speaking to a holomorph. The visual illusion was perfect, only betrayed by a slight studio quality to the voice. It had been beamed at Dallen's ears too accurately, robbing it of any acoustic interaction with the considerable volume of sound coming from rooms on either side of the hall.

"In that case let me introduce myself," the holomorph said. "I am Karal London, and I offer you some wonderful news—you, my friend, are going to live for ever."

"Is that a fact?" Dallen replied uneasily, loathe to converse with the unseen computer which was directing the holomorph's responses.

"Not only is it a fact, my friend—it is the single most important truth in the cosmos. You will have ample opportunity to discuss it during the evening—and there is a comprehensive range of study aids, all available to you free of charge—but let me begin by asking you one vital question. What is . . ?"

The question was lost to Dallen as the door at his right opened and the bouyantly curvacious figure of Rick Renard appeared, martini glass in hand. He grinned on seeing Dallen, walked straight to the holomorph and shoved his knee into the vicinity of its groin.

"Out of the way, you silly old fart," he commanded, stepping into the solid image and causing it to flow and fragment. "This really balls the whole system. Old Karal programmed the set-up himself before he left for Orbitsville, but he was too conceited to allow for anybody being disrespectful enough to stand right inside him. The computer just doesn't know how to react."

"I'm not surprised," Dallen said, reluctantly amused.

"Wait to you see this." Renard edged backwards a

little, allowing London's image to reassemble itself in front of him, now apparently with four arms, two of which belonged to Renard and were waving like those of a Balinese dancer.

". . . long been postulated that mind is a universal property of matter, so that even elementary particles would be endowed with it to some degree," the grotesque image was saying in London's voice. "We now know that mind is a universal entity or interaction of the same order as electricity or gravitation, and that there exists a modulus of transformation, analogous to Einstein's basic equation, which equates mind stuff with other entities of the physical world . . ."

The superimposed image abruptly vanished, leaving the floor to a triumphant Renard. "The programme can't cope, you see. Old Karal should have stuck to his physics."

"He didn't expect sabotage."

"What *did* he expect? People come here for some free booze and a bit of discreet lusting after Silvia—not to be lectured by a miserable bloody apparition. Come on, old son, you look as though you could use a drink."

"It's been one of those days."

"Yeah." Renard paused, his gold-freckled face looking uncharacteristically solemn. "I've only just heard about your wife and kid."

"I don't want to talk about that."

"No. It was just that I . . . Ah, *hell!*" Renard led the way into the room from which he had emerged and went to a long sideboard which was serving as a bar. Dallen asked him for a weak Scotch and water, and while it was being prepared took the opportunity to look around. There were about two dozen people

in the room, most of them men, who were standing
in groups of three or four. He recognised several
faces from various City Hall departments, but was
unable to see Silvia.

"She's around somewhere," Renard said knowingly,
flashing his narrow bow of teeth.

Dallen concealed his annoyance over having his
screens penetrated so easily. "Why are these people
here? They can't all be theoretical physicists."

"Metaphysicists would be more like it. Karal claims
there are special particles called mindons which are
harder to detect than neutrinos because they exist in
what he calls mental space. It's all a bit abstruse for a
mere botanist, but apparently our brains have mindon
look-alikes in mental space—where most of the physical laws are different—which enable us to survive
death. Karal doesn't talk about dying—he refers to it
as becoming discarnate.

"It's all supposed to be very comforting and
uplifting," Renard added as he handed Dallen a clink-
ing glass. "Personally, I prefer this stuff or an occasional dab of jinks."

"Felicitin?" Dallen was only mildly curious. "Can
you get it right here in Madison?"

Renard shrugged. "A dealer comes through from
the west coast once a month, so somebody in town
must be really hooked on the stuff."

"Who's got that kind of money?"

"Dealers don't talk. Felicitin isn't illegal, as you
know, but heavy users generally get up to some
highly illegal activities sooner or later. You can sometimes spot them, though, if you know what to look
for."

Dallen sipped his drink and was a little surprised

to find it had been mixed exactly to his specification. Renard was on his best behaviour. *How*, he wondered, *would you pinpoint a person who was really dosing up on felicitin? Look out for someone who was always cool and calm, exuding that air of serene confidence . . ?* A memory picture flickered briefly behind his eyes—tall young man with Nordic good looks, expensively tailored, relaxed, smiling. Dallen concentrated until he had identified the image as that of Gerald Mathieu, the deputy mayor, then frowned and peered into his glass as a coldness developed in his stomach.

"I hope this isn't supercooled ice," he said. "I've heard this stuff can be bad for you."

Renard smiled. "It's always the ice—never the booze."

Dallen nodded, becoming aware of a man and woman purposefully moving closer to him. He turned and saw the rotund figure of Peter Ezzati, the city's salvage officer, accompanied by his equally plump wife, Libby. While they were shaking hands he noticed that the woman's eyes were following his with a kind of melting intensity and he guessed with a sinking feeling that she was a tragedy buff, a professional sympathiser.

"Is this your first time here, Garry?" Ezzati said. "Are you enjoying it?"

"I'm a bit vague about what I'm supposed to enjoy."

"The talk, mainly. Karal can be quite convincing about his mindons, if you follow his argument right through, but it's the conversation I like. You get guys here whose minds aren't limited to sport and sex, who can talk about *anything*. For instance, what do you think about these green flashes they're getting on Orbitsville?"

Dallen was baffled. "I'm afraid I . . ."

"You're the first policeman we've had at the meetings," Libby Ezzati put in, her gaze still a channel for moist compassion.

"I'm not a policeman," Dallen explained. "I work for the Deregistration Bureau."

Libby shot an accusing glance at her husband, as though charging him with having told her lies. "But you can arrest people, can't you?"

"Only for things like being on land where there's an exclusion order in force."

"That's another thing," Ezzati said. "Is it true they're pulling the deregister line in to a forty kilometre radius of Madison?"

Dallen nodded. "The population here is shrinking. There's enough good farming land within the radius."

"I don't like it—it's all part of a process." Ezzati considered what he had just said and appeared to find it significant. "All part of a process."

"Everything is part of a process," Dallen said.

"I'm not talking philosophy—I'm talking people."

"You're talking piffle, darling," Libby told her husband, and having allied herself with Dallen decided it was rapport time. "You know, Garry, Kipling had a vital message for all of us when he pointed out that God never wasted a leaf or a tree . . ."

"Rick is the botanist around here." Dallen walked away quickly and went back into the hall where the rematerialised holomorph of Karal London was addressing two new arrivals . . . *discarnate mind composed of mindons interacts with matter only very weakly, but that doesn't call its existence into question. After all, we have yet to detect the graviton or the gravitino . . .* Coming out of the beam of sound, Dallen went into the room opposite and found it populated like the one he had left, small groups standing and talking earnestly in an ambience of low-placed lights and amber drinks.

He worked his way through them and went into the extension where yesterday morning, which seemed an aeon ago, he had first seen Silvia's incredible glass mosaic screen. The studio was empty. Diffuser lamps were shining behind the trefoil panels, providing a patchy illumination which obscured the design of the three universes, shading them off into a mysterious darkness suggestive of the vast tracts of the cosmos beyond the limits of human vision. Dallen found the entire construct beautiful beyond words, and again he was awed by the sheer amount of labour that it represented. His appreciation of art was untutored, a chief criterion being that a piece should appear difficult, to have taxed the artist's powers, to have been hard work—and by that standard alone the screen, with its hundreds of thousands of varicoloured glass chips, had to be the most impressive and soul-glutting creation he had ever seen.

"It's not for sale," Silvia London said from close behind him.

"Pity—I was going to commission a dozen." He turned and found himself warmed by her presence. Everything about her seemed *right* to him—the humorous intelligence in the brown eyes, the determination of the chin, the strength combined with the utter femininity of the fullbosomed figure sheathed in a pleated white dress.

"Perhaps I could make you a little suncatcher," she said.

"It wouldn't be the same. Being little, I mean. It's

the size of this thing—all those separate pieces of
glass—which helps make it what it is."

Silvia's lips twitched. "You're a dialectical material-
ist."

"Step outside and say that," Dallen challenged.
Silvia laughed and this time his arms, unbidden,
actually opened a little to receive her. He froze in a
turmoil of guilt and confusion. Silvia seemed to catch
her breath and her eyes became troubled.

"I was talking to Rick a little while ago," she said.
"He told me what happened to your family. I'd heard
about it before, but I didn't realise . . . I didn't connect you . . ."

"It's all right. It's my problem."

She nodded thoughtfully. "I've heard of people
making a full recovery."

"It depends on how close they were to the gun. If
only the memory cells are affected it's possible for a
person to be re-educated, recreated almost, in a year
or so, because all the connecting networks that person built up are still intact. But if the cell connections
have been damaged . . ."

Dallen hesitated, shocked at finding himself discussing the subject with an outsider, and even more so
by what he was about to admit to himself. "Cona and
Mikel were hit at very close range. I think they're
gone."

"I'm so sorry." Silvia stared at him for a moment,
shoulders slightly raised, as if coming to a decision.
"Garry, I'm not trying to push Karal's ideas at you,
but there's something I'd like you to see. Will you
come and look?"

"I don't mind," He said, setting his glass down.

"Through here." Silvia led the way to the back of

the studio, into a workshop which was equipped with a range of machine tools, and from there into a short corridor. At the end of it was a heavy door which she opened by thumbprinting the lock. Revealed was a large square chamber which was dominated by a rectangular transparent box resembling a display case in a museum. Suspended inside the box on near-invisible wires were six spheres of polished alloy roughly a metre in diameter. Dallen went closer to the case and saw that each sphere was surrounded by a cluster of delicate needle-like probes, all of them impinging in a direction normal to the surface. Wires from the bases of the probes converged on instrument housings on the floor beneath the case.

"Impressive," Dallen said. "I've seen a Newton's cradle before, but not his double bed."

"My husband and five other volunteers are surrendering their lives for this experiment," Silvia replied, making it clear that flippancy was not welcome. "The probes are not actually touching the spheres, though it looks that way. The tip of each one is ten microns from the surface. They're kept at that distance by sensors and microcontrols even if the spheres are disturbed by local vibrations or earth tremors or temperature changes. The system compensates for all natural forces."

"What's the point of it?"

Silvia's face was solemn. "It won't compensate for supranatural forces. Karal is planning to move the first sphere in the line when he becomes discarnate. If he is successful, as he fully expects to be, the sphere will make contact with one or more probes, and there'll be a signal."

"I see." Dallen sought a way to conceal his instinctive scepticism. "Proof of life after death."

"Proof that what we call death is merely a transition."

Dallen realised that he had to be honest. "Haven't other people tried to send signals back from the quote other side unquote?"

"They weren't physicists with a full understanding of quantum non-location and the forces involved."

"No, but . . . I never heard of mindons before tonight, but I gather that if they exist at all their interaction with matter is very, very weak. How could a . . . discarnate entity composed of mindons hope to move a thing like that?" Dallen flicked his thumb to indicate the nearest of the massive spheres.

"Karal teaches that mindons are somehow related to gravitons."

"But we don't even know that gravitons exist."

"But, but, but!" Silvia's smile was sadly messianic. "Has it ever struck you how onomatopoeic that word is?"

"I'm in a constant state of wonderment over it," Dallen said and immediately cursed the verbal reflex which often tricked him into hurting those he had no wish to hurt, but Silvia was unaffected.

She went straight into a discourse on nuclear physics, the gist of which was that not all fundamental interactions are common to all particles—a neutrino having just one—which opened the theoretical door for mindons having only the mental interaction plus another, as yet undemonstrated, with gravitons. The picture Dallen received was one of a dead Karal London somehow riding herd on a swarm of gravitons and guiding them across interstellar space to collide with one of the six spheres. He also gleaned that there were five other elderly disciples—one on Orbitsville, one on the planet Terranova, three in various parts of Earth—who had similar visionary plans, each with a separate sphere as his target. It was a scenario which Dallen found quite preposterous.

"I'm sorry," he said. "It's too much for me. I can't believe it."

"Belief isn't necessary at this stage—all you have to do is accept that it's all conceivable in terms of present day physics." Silvia spoke as one repeating a creed. "A personality is a structure of mental entities, existing in mental space, and it survives destruction of the brain even though it required the brain's complex physical organisation in order to develop."

"My brain is getting a bit overheated," Dallen said, dabbing imaginary sweat from his brow.

"All right—here endeth the first lesson—but I warn you you'll get more of the same when you come back." Silvia walked to the door of the chamber and paused for him to join her. "*If* you come back."

"I don't scare easily." *You liar*, he told himself, *you're going weak at the knees*. He was acutely aware as he walked towards her that a clearly delineated "business" phase of the encounter had ended, that they were alone, and that she was waiting in the actual doorway, which meant there would be a moment in which it would be almost impossible to avoid contact. He went to her and an instinct prompted him to extend his hands, palm outwards and fingers slightly apart, in a gesture which had meaning only for the two of them and only for that unique instant. Silvia put her hands against his, interlocking their fingers, and the warmth of her entered him and changed him. He tried to move closer, but she checked him with a slight increase of pressure.

"Don't kiss me, Garry," she said. "I couldn't handle it."

"Does that mean it's too soon?"

She eyed him soberly. "I think that's what it means."

"In that case," he said, deciding that a change of mood would be good strategy, "shall we repair to wherever people repair at a time like this?"

Silvia nodded, looking grateful, and they walked back through the studio to the main part of the house, where she parted from him to attend other guests. Dallen's feeling of elation lasted perhaps five seconds after she was lost to view, and then—as he had known it would—there came a reaction. The predominant emotion was guilt, his constant companion in recent weeks, but now a caustic new element had been added, one he had trouble identifying. Was it in the acknowledgement of what Silvia London could do to him, his belated discovery of the difference between affection, which he had always assumed to be love, and another kind of emotion altogether—wayward and unsettling—which might really be love?"

I ought to get out of here, he thought. *I ought to get out of here right now and never come back.* He turned to walk to the door and almost collided with Peter Ezzati and his wife.

"You've been getting your indoctrination," Ezzati said gleefully. "I can tell by your face."

"Peter!" Libby was overtly tactful. "Garry doesn't want intrusions."

Dallen looked down at her, recalled his earlier lack of manners and forced a smile. "I'm afraid I get a bit irritable when it's past my bedtime—I must need a cocoa infusion or something."

"I'll get you a proper drink," Ezzati said, moving away. "Scotch and water, wasn't it?"

Dallen considered calling him back and refusing the drink and leaving immediately, then came the realisation that it was still only around ten in the evening and his chances of sleeping if he went back to his empty house were zero. It could be a good idea to spend some time with neutral and undemanding people, to wind down a little and prove to himself that he was a balanced and mature person with complete control over his emotions.

"I was reading a bit about probability math the other day," he said, seeking total irrelevancy. "It said that if two people lose each other in a big department store there's no guarantee they'll *ever* meet up again unless one of them stands still."

An expression of polite bafflement appeared on Libby's round face. "How interesting."

"Yes, but if you think about it that has to be one of the most useless pieces of information ever. I mean . . ."

"I've never been to a big department store," Libby said. "It must have been wonderful to visit somewhere like Macy's before they let New York go down. Something else that's been lost . . ."

Dallen was unable to produce an original comment. "You win some, you lose some."

"If that were the case things might be reasonable, but the fact is that we lose, lose, lose. Optima Thule has taken everything and given nothing back."

In spite of his emotional disquiet, Dallen was able to interest himself in the point of view. "Aren't we taking from Optima Thule? Isn't it doing all the giving?"

"I'm not talking about patches of grass. What has the human race *done* in the last two centuries? Nothing! There has been practically no progress in any of the arts. Science is static. Technology is actually slipping back a notch or two every year. Orbitsville is a *sink!*"

"This seems to be my lecture night," Dallen said.

"I'm sorry." Libby gave him a rueful smile and he realised he had been too quick to categorise her earlier. "I'm a romantic, you see, and for me Orbitsville is an ending, not a beginning. I can't help wondering what Garamond and all the others would have found if Orbitsville hadn't been there and they had kept on going."

"Probably nothing."

"Probably, but now we'll never know. There's a galaxy out there, and we turned our backs on it. Sometimes, when I'm feeling paranoic, I suspect that Orbitsville was built for that very reason."

"Orbitsville wasn't built by anybody," Dallen said. "Only people who have never been there can think of it as an artifact. When you've actually seen the oceans and the mountains and the . . ." He broke off as Ezzati appeared at his side and thrust a full glass into his hand with unnecessary vigour.

"Some of these guys have a bloody nerve," Ezzati muttered, his apple cheeks dark with anger. "I'm doing no more favours, folks—not for anybody."

Libby was immediately sympathetic. "What happened?"

"That young weasel Solly Hume, that's what happened! He's getting tanked up in the next room, and when I hinted to him—purely for his own good, mind you—that he was overdoing it a bit he had the gall to say I owed him fifty monits."

"Peter, you haven't been borrowing," Libby said, looking concerned.

"Try to talk sense, will you?" Ezzati gulped down some liquor and concentrated his attention on Dallen. "Last week I practically *gave* that kid Hume an obsolete computer for his stupid bloody society, and tonight he had the nerve to ask for his money back. Said its guts had been denatured or something like that. What does he expect from a gizmo that's been lying in a basement since the year dot?"

"Perhaps he thought it would have glass tubes," Dallen said, wishing his own problems could be so trivial. "You know—hollow state technology."

"No, it's only an old Department of Supply monitor he found on Sublevel Three. There used to be a computer centre down there. Apparently this thing was supposed to keep tabs on municipal supplies. It beats me why anybody would want to be bothered with it."

Dallen felt the coolness return to his system, as if a door was swinging ajar.

"You've argued yourself into a corner, darling," Libby said scornfully. "If the monitor was so boring and useless in the first place you were lucky to get fifty monits for it."

"Yes, but . . ." Ezzati glared at her, unwilling to concede the point. "I'll take it back from Hume and advertise it properly. Electronic archaeology is a big thing these days, you know. As a matter of fact . . ." He frowned into his glass as he swirled its contents. ". . . I might already have another customer. I seem to remember somebody else asking me about that machine."

"Now you're being childish," Libby said, her voice vibrant with scorn. "Admit it."

Dallen stared frozenly at Ezzati, willing him to produce a name.

"Perhaps you're right," Ezzati said with a shrug. "Why should I get worked up when it isn't my money that's involved? You don't get any credit for bringing the job home with you. Not around here, anyway. There was a time when I was dumb enough to believe that all it took to get a man to the top in Madison was hard work and dedication and loyalty, then I got wise to myself and . . . Gerald Mathieu!"

"You got wise to yourself and Gerald Mathieu?" Libby stared at him, feigning concern, and raised her gaze to Dallen's face. "Have you any idea what my idiot husband is talking about?"

"I'm afraid he has lost me," Dallen said, moving away in search of a place where he could be alone with his thoughts, where he could begin to draw up his plans.

Chapter 11

There were now only two aircraft at the disposal of Madison City's executive board, and one of them had been grounded for more than a week pending the arrival of parts. Mayor Bryceland was inclined to treat the remaining machine as his personal transport, with the result that it had taken Mathieu four anxious days to get behind its controls. He had one decent fix of felicitin in hand, but had been rationing his usuage severely to obtain that slender reserve. As he fastened down the aircraft's canopy he felt tired and apprehensive, almost certain there would be a last-minute hitch to prevent his taking off.

Far off to his right, its lower surface obscured by heat shimmers, was the blue-and-white hull of a space shuttle which had just landed. The churning of the hot air above the expanse of ferrocrete was so violent that Mathieu had difficulty in seeing the disembarking tourists, but it seemed to him that there were less than usual. It had already been a bad year for the hotels along Farewell Avenue—the thoroughfare which

had once channeled millions of emigrants into space—
and it looked as though things were going to get
worse. There had to come a day, Mathieu realised,
when the remote bureaucrats of Optima Thule would
pull out the plug and stop subsidising the holiday
pilgrimages to Earth. And when that happened he
would be out of a job and would have to consider
returning to his birthplace.

The thought of venturing out among the stars, of
having to spend the rest of his life on the surface of an
incredibly flimsy bubble, brought the usual stab of
agoraphobic dread. He began to reach for the gold
pen in his inner pocket, became aware of what he
was doing and returned his hand to the aircraft's
control column. Far ahead of him, a quivering silvery
blur at the lower edge of the sky's blue dome, was a
freighter coming in from Metagov Central Clearing in
Winnipeg. It gradually drifted off to one side and the
on-board microprocessor advised Mathieu that it was
in order for him to begin the flight.

Deciding to do the work himself, he extended the
aircraft's invisible wings to take-off configuration and
increased the thrust from its drive tubes. In a matter
of seconds he was soaring above the complex of dis-
used runways which constituted most of Madison
Field. He banked to the west and levelled off at only
a hundred metres, aiming at the serried green ridges
which were the southernmost reaches of the Appala-
chians. The ship's shadow raced beneath him, fringed
with prismatics from sunlight which had become
entangled in force-field wings.

It came to Mathieu that this was his first time to be
airborne since the City Hall incident . . . *woman and
child, crumpling, plastic doll faces with plastic doll eyes* . . .

and that he was deriving none of his customary satisfaction from the experience. Flying fast and low on manual control over the empty countryside had been one of his most biding pleasures, the perfect escape from all the pressures of identity, but on this summer morning his problems were easily keeping pace, like invisible wingmen.

The pay-offs he had to make to run his illegal business were growing at a frightening rate, his work was suffering, women friends were reacting badly to changes in his temperment, and—looming above all else—was the responsibility for having extinguished two human personalities. There was the associated guilt . . . and the consequent fear of Garry Dallen, which felicitin could only allay for short periods . . . and it was hard to say which was casting the greater pall over his existence. And he had become so very, *very* tired . . .

Mathieu opened his eyes and stared at the green wall of hillside which was tilting and expanding directly ahead of him, filling his field of view.

Christ, I'm going to die!

He shouted a curse as he realised where he was and what was happening to him. His hands pulled back on the control column, but the hillside kept coming at him, huge and solid and lethal, determined to reduce his body to a crimson slurry. It was aided and abetted by the laws of aerodynamics which imposed a lag between a control demand and the ship's response, and he knew only too well that the penalty for acting too late was death.

Mathieu cringed back in the seat, eyes distended and mouth agape, as the expansion of the hillside speeded up to become a green explosion. The control column was back to its full extent, punishing the shuddering airframe, calling on the ship to do the impossible—then an edge of sky appeared.

The horizon rocked and fell away beneath the ship's prow.

For perhaps a minute Mathieu sat mouthing swear words, stringing them into a meaningless chant while his heart lurched and thudded like a runaway motor which was tearing itself from its mountings. Only when his breathing had returned to normal and the prickling of cold sweat had died away from his forehead and palms was he able to relax, but even then he did not feel quite safe. He glanced around the quiet-droning environment of the cockpit and had actually begun to check his instruments when it dawned on him that the new threat, the new source of danger, was in his own mind.

An idea had been implanted, one which had been conceived during the brush with oblivion. For a single instant, in the midst of all the prayer and panic, there had been the temptation—strange, sweet and shameful—to push *forward* on the stick. In that split-second he could almost have gone willingly to his death, riding the crest of a dark wave.

Mathieu tried to consider the notion dispassionately. It was shocking and unnatural to him, and at the same time it was strangely beguiling, full of intriguing contradictions.

He had no wish to die—but he was attracted by the prospect of being dead.

A state of non-existence had many advantages. There would be no more nightmares and no more of the terrible waking visions. There would be no guilt or fear. There would be no need to steal, no need to finance his habit. There would be no need to lie or to hide. There would be no need to go on and on tricking people into believing he was what he appeared to be.

There would be no need to fear going into space or the prospect having to face the dizzy vastness of Orbitsville. There would be no need to dread failure.

There would be no future and no past. In short, there would be no Gerald Mathieu, the man who only existed as a compound of failure. And as a special bonus, one he could claim immediately, there would be no need to hold at bay the tiredness which had begun to follow him everywhere like a stalking animal.

That was perhaps the most seductive aspect of the idea. He could start right away by closing his eyes for a short period, say for one minute, just to see what happened and how he felt about it. There did not have to be any great melodramatic decision to commit suicide—it was more like a game, or an experiment which could be terminated at any point he chose . . .

Mathieu glanced at his airspeed indicator and saw that he was doing almost a thousand kilometres an hour. *Nice round figure*, he thought. He relaxed his grip on the yoke, closed his eyes and began to count off the seconds. At once he became aware of the low-amplitude hum of the power plant and the rush of atmosphere along the pressure skin. The ship was suddenly alive, yawing and twisting and dancing, impossibly balanced on an invisible pyramid of air.

On the count of only twelve Mathieu snapped his eyelids open and found he was still flying straight and level. The universe was unchanged—a blueness of prehistoric purity above and all around him, vivid grasslands streaming below the ship's nose, occasional farm buildings smothered in vegetation, fleeting targets for his imaginary World War Two cannon.

It's risky flying at this height, he told himself. *A man could get killed.*

He took a deep breath, blinked to clear his eyes, and gave the task of flying his full attention, wondering if he would ever again summon up the courage for the great gamble. The aircraft butted and squirmed its way through a patch of turbulence, then settled down to quiet sensationless flight. It was hot in the cockpit and the sun seemed to be exerting a gentle downward pressure on his eyelids.

Mathieu resisted it for several minutes before deciding there would be no harm, no real danger, in shutting his eyes for a mere ten seconds. It was, after all, just a game.

There was no blackness when he closed his eyes—only a pink infinity swarming with magenta and green after-images. He reached the count of ten easily and decided to try for twenty. *If I fell asleep now Garry Dallen would never be able to touch me. I'm not going to sleep, of course, but it would be so good to stop running up those concrete stairs, to stop pulling the trigger on the woman and child, to stop seeing them crumpling, falling, idiot eyes staring . . .*

An angry bleeping from the control console told Mathieu important changes were taking place in the outside universe, changes he ought to know about.

But he waited another five seconds before opening his eyes, and by then it was possible to distinguish separate blades of grass on the hillside which filled the entire field of view ahead.

He had time for one flicker of gratitude over the fact that there was absolutely nothing he could do.

It was easy, he thought, in the instant of the plane becoming a bomb.

Easy as

Chapter 12

The planning of a murder presented special difficulties, Dallen had realised.

Among them were the sheer novelty of the problem parameters and the ingrained moral objections which constantly disrupted his chains of thought. *But this can't be me*, the jolting recrimination would run, *I just don't do this kind of thing*. There was also the overriding need to make the murder look like an accidental death. An obvious homicide would trigger an investigation which was certain to reveal the circumstances which had led to Mathieu's fateful encounter with Cona and Mikel Dallen in the quietness of the north stairwell—and from there a short step in elementary police logic would lead to Garry Dallen.

The subsequent punishment would be little in itself. Dallen did not even regard a one-way trip to Orbitsville's Botany Bay as a punishment—which was partly why he could not allow Gerald Mathieu to escape along that road—but it would separate him from Cona and Mikel, thereby adding to the hurt they had al-

ready suffered. There was only one way for the issue
to be resolved. Mathieu would have to die, preferrably
in a way he fully understood to be an execution, but
which would appear like an accident to all others.
And therein lay the practical difficulties.

Edgy and preoccupied, Dallen wandered into the
kitchen and found Betti Knopp preparing lunch. She
was a middle-aged voluntary worker who came to the
house three days a week to shoulder the burden of
looking after Cona, a duty she performed conscien-
tiously and in almost total silence. Dallen was grateful to her, but had not managed to build any kind of
conversational bridge. Aware of her uneasiness over
his presence in the kitchen, he excused himself and
went into the main room. Cona was standing at the
window, looking out at the sloping perspectives of
the North Hill. Her hair had been combed and neatly
arranged in an adult style by Betti, and her attitude
was one of wistful contemplation, just as in the period of homesickness following her arrival from
Orbitsville.

Dallen was tempted to indulge in fantasy—the past
weeks had been nothing more than a nightmare and
Cona was her old self. He went to the window and
put his arms around her. She turned and snuggled
against him, making a cooing sound of pleasure and
only the smell of chocolate, which the old Cona
always avoided, interfered with the illusion that somehow his wife had been restored to him. He stared
over her head in the direction of Madison's City Hall,
unable to stop dashing his mind against the barriers
of the past. If only he had not arranged to have lunch
with Cona that day. If only he had been in his office.
If only she had gone in by the main entrance. If only

Mathieu had blanked the Department of Supply monitor a day or an hour or a minute later or earlier . . .

Dallen gave a low grunt of surprise as he discovered that Cona had cupped her hand on his genitals and was beginning to massage him with clumsy eagerness. For a second he almost yielded, then self-disgust plumed through him and he stepped back abruptly. Cona came after him, giggling, her gaze fixed on his groin.

"Don't do that," he snapped, holding her at arm's length. "No, Cona, no!"

She raised her eyes, reacting to the denial in his voice, and her face distored into ugliness in a baby grimace of rage. She went for him again, strong and uninhibited, and he had to struggle to hold her in check. At that moment Betti Knopp came into the room with a tray of food. She gave Dallen a worried glance and turned to leave.

"Bring it," he ordered, pushing Cona down into an armchair. The sudden force he had to use either hurt or alarmed her and she gave a loud sob which in turn drew a gasp from Betti, the first sound he had heard her make that day. She knelt by Cona and attracted her attention by noisily stirring a dish of something yellow and glutinous. Dallen stared helplessly at the two women, then strode to the other end of the room and activated the holovision set.

"Speak to me, please," he said to the solid image of a thin, silver-bearded man which appeared at the set's focus. Dallen had dropped into a chair and folded his arms across his chest before realising the image was that of Karal London. He leaned forward intently.

". . . was in his early sixties," a news reader was

saying, "and is understood to have refused treatment for the lung condition which led to his death. Doctor London was best known in the Madison City area as a philanthropist and creator of the Anima Mundi Foundation, an organisation devoted to promoting an exotic blend of science and religion. It was his work for the Foundation which took him to Optima Thule two years ago, and today there are unconfirmed reports that a bizarre experiment—designed by Doctor London to prove some of his theories—has been . . ."

"Mister Dallen!" Betti Knopp appeared directly in front of him as if by magic, hands on hips, elbows stuck out in the classic posture of exasperation. "There's something we have to get straight."

He said, "Wait a minute—I'm trying to hear what . . ."

"I *won't* wait a minute—you're going to hear me out right now!" Betti, who had been almost totally silent for weeks, was transformed into a noise-making machine. "I don't have to take all this high-and-mighty treatment from you or anybody else."

"Please let me hear this one item, and then we'll . . ."

"If you think you're too important to talk with me why don't you contact the clinic and see if they got somebody more to your taste? Why don't you?"

Dallen got to his feet, tried to placate Betti and only succeeded in attracting the attention of Cona, who added to the noise level by starting to pound on her tray with a dish. He turned and ran upstairs to his bedroom, slammed the door shut behind him and switched on another holovision. The local newscast was still running, but now the subject was hotel closures. He tried to activate the set's ten-minute memory facility and swore silently but fervently as he remembered it needed repair. Tense with frustration, he considered returning to the downstairs set, then came an abrupt shift to a more analytical mode of thought.

It had been established that Karal London was dead, so the big question troubling Dallen related to the strange experiment. Was the fact of its being mentioned at all an indication that there had been a surprising result?

The notion seemed more preposterous than ever—the idea of a deceased scientist reaching out across the light years from Orbitsville and disturbing a material object on Earth—but why were the information media interested? Would anybody connected with the Anima Mundi Foundation have been in a hurry to spread word of a negative result?

And why, he thought in a conflict of emotion, *am I standing around here?*

There were five cars already parked on the gravel in front of the London place, and among them—inevitably it seemed—was Renard's gold Rollac. The front door of the house was open. Dallen went inside, found the hall deserted, and turned left to walk through the living room and the studio beyond. Afternoon sunlight had transformed the fantastic glass mosaic into a curtain of varicoloured fire. Dallen hurried past it and made his way to the corridor which ran towards the rear of the premises, following a murmur of voices. He reached the chamber housing the experimental apparatus and found the door ajar.

In the dimness beyond were perhaps a dozen people in a rough circle about the case containing the six metal spheres. As his eyes adjusted to the conditions

Dallen made out the white-clad figure of Silvia London, with Renard standing next to her. She was slightly stooped and was hugging herself as though trying to ward off coldness. Dallen knew she had been crying. He paused in the doorway, uncertain of his right to enter, until Renard beckoned to him.

Feeling conspicuous, he moved forward a few paces and joined the circle of watchers whose attention was fixed on the first sphere in the row of six. A lengthy silence ensued and he felt a growing disappointment, a sense of anticlimax. It was apparent to him now that the members of the group were still waiting for a sign, for proof that their mentor continued to exist as an entity composed of virtually undetectable particles.

Naivety of that magnitude, he supposed, would in itself be a newsworthy item, and he too was guilty in that respect, otherwise he would still be at home. Or would he? He had discovered that his unconscious mind possessed neither scruples nor pride, so it was quite possible that he had come to the London house quite simply to be seen by Silvia as soon as possible after her husband's death—a tactic his conscious mind could only despise.

Irritated by yet another plunge into self-analysis, Dallen looked for an unobtrusive means of escape from the circle, but even Renard was displaying a kind of reverent absorption in the gleaming sphere and its matrix of sensors. *Playing up to Silvia now that Karal is out of the way?* The sheer adolescent bitchiness of the thought sparked Dallen's annoyance with himself into full-blown anger.

He turned to walk out—and in the same instant a blue lumitube above the first sphere flickered into life.

It glowed for several seconds, during which the silence in the chamber was like grey glass, then the light faded. The silence was disrupted by near-explosive sighs followed immediately by the clamour of voices. Somebody gave a quavering but triumphant laugh. Dallen continued to stare at the polished sphere while he tried to rebuild his private view of the universe.

If the brief wash of photons from the lumitube meant what it was supposed to mean, Karal London was actually in the same room with him, occupying the same space. The imputation was that, released from his body by death, the physicist had been able to rove out across interstellar space and by some unimaginable means impose his will on the forces of gravity.

The message was that the human personality could survive dissolution of the body, had the potential for immortality.

Dallen felt a stealthy chill move down his spine and he shivered. Could he now believe that the Cona Dallen to whom he had been married also still existed in another kind of space? Or would London's theory have it that the assault on her physical brain had to be equally destructive to a mindon counterpart? But that implied . . .

"I'm a victim of philosophical rape," Renard whispered, appearing at Dallen's side. "Old Karal has screwed up at least half of my highly expensive education."

Dallen nodded, his gaze fixed on Silvia who was leaving the chamber amid a knot of men and women, all of whom were speaking to her at once. "Where's everybody going? Don't they want to wait and see if anything else happens?"

"Nothing more is expected—that was the fifth signal. Didn't Silvia mention that bit? It's all part of Karal's experimental procedure. As well as having a separate target, each volunteer is supposed to send a different number of pulses." Speaking in a low voice, with none of his customary scoffing vulgarity, Renard explained that the first signal had been detected four hours previously. On receiving it Silvia had notified some officers of the Foundation and, in accordance with an agreed plan, they had sent a tachygram to Karal London's residence in Port Napier, Orbitsville. There had come immediate confirmation that London had just died. For most workers in the field of the paranormal that would have been sufficient proof of the theory, but London had wanted to go further. The arrival of a predetermined number of signals would, as well as being a powerful argument against a freak equipment malfunction, demonstrate that in his discarnate form he could reproduce familiar human thought patterns. It would also show that time in mental space was compatible with time in normal space.

"I hate to admit it," Renard concluded, "but I owe the good Doctor London an apology."

"Aren't you a bit late?"

"Not at all." Renard faced the now empty chamber and spread his arms. "Karal, you old bugger, you're not as crazy as you look."

"Very handsome apology," Dallen said.

"The least I could do, old son—it isn't every day that somebody is obliging enough to die and leave you his wife. Did I mention that Silvia is going to the Big O with me?"

Dallen's heart sledged against his ribs. "It must have slipped your mind."

"Beautiful self-control, Garry—you didn't even blink." Renard's arch of teeth glinted as he peered into Dallen's face. "The Foundation's main job now is to spread the glad tidings, which means there's no point in Silvia hanging around here when somebody else can keep an eye on the experiment. All the scientific bodies have their headquarters on Orbitsville, so . . ."

"Will she address them herself?"

"Only as a figurehead—and that's a job she's really cut out for. There'll be some qualified physicists from the Foundation going out to do all the talking, and I'm giving everybody a free trip." Renard smiled again. "Just to prove what a genuinely decent person I am."

"Of course." Determined not to become involved in any of Renard's private games, Dallen began to leave.

"Wait a minute, Garry." Renard moved to block the doorway. "Why don't you go back to Orbitsville with us? There's nothing on this clapped-out ball of mud for you or your family. I've got most of my grass specimens on board the ship and we'll be ready to go in a couple of days."

"Thanks, but I'm not interested."

"Free trip, old son. And no delays. Worth thinking about."

Dallen repressed a pang of dislike. "If I asked why you wanted me along, would you give me a straight answer?"

"A *straight* answer? What an unreasonable request!" The humorous glint faded from Renard's eyes. "Would you believe that I just like you and want to help?"

"Try something else."

"Garry, you shouldn't be so unbending. What if I say it's because you're the nearest thing I have to a rival? I told you before that the universe looks after me and gives me everything I want, which is fine— but it gets a bit boring. I mean, I *know* I'm going to have Silvia . . . I can't lose . . . but if you were around there'd be the illusion of competition, and it would make life more interesting for all concerned. How does that sound?"

"It sounds weird," Dallen said. "Are you on felicitin right now?"

Renard shook his head. "I'm naturally like this— and I'm not letting you out of here until you agree that we're all going to Orbitsville together."

"That's an infringement of my liberty." Dallen smiled pleasantly, masking the glandular spurting which accompanied the thought of being allowed to put his hands on Renard. He had taken one step towards him when a confusion of sounds reached them from another part of the building—startled voices, an irregular hammering, the shattering of glass. Renard turned and walked quickly along the corridor with Dallen at his heels. A rapid increase in the noise level told them the commotion was originating in the studio section. The repeated splintering of glass gave Dallen a sick premonition.

He entered the studio at a run and had to edge through a cluster of people to see what was happening. Their attention was concentrated on Silvia. She was gripping a long metal bar and was using it, swinging from one side and then the other, to destroy her glass mosaic screen.

At each slicing impact another part of the unique creation ruptured and sagged, and brilliant motes of colour sprayed like water droplets. Galaxies and clusters of galaxies were annihilated at every stroke. Silvia laboured like an automaton, hewing and clubbing, sobbing aloud each time she overcame the inertia of the heavy bar. Her face was white, the eyes Samson-blind to the transient bright-hued fountains she was creating.

Four years' work and a third of a million pieces of glass, Dallen recited in his head in a kind of dismayed chant. *Please don't erase your own life*.

He wanted to dart forward and bring the destruction to an end, but was paralysed by a curious timidity, a fear of intruding on private torment. All he could do was stand and watch until Silvia's strength failed. She raised the bar high, aiming for the uppermost part of the trefoil design, but it wavered and circled in her grasp and she had to let it fall. She stood for a moment, head bowed, before turning to face the group.

"It was a memorial," she said in a dazed, abstracted voice. "Karal doesn't need a memorial. He isn't dead." She stared at Dallen, breathing hard, and took a half-step in his direction.

"You're coming with me," said Libby Ezzati as she stepped forward and put a motherly arm around Silvia's shoulders. "You're going to lie down."

"It's the best thing," agreed Peter Ezzati, apparently having just arrived at the house. His rotund body was encased in a dark formal suit to which he had added a band of black crêpe on one arm. He positioned himself beside Silvia to help usher her out of the studio and recoiled, comically startled, when she clawed at his armband.

"Take that bloody thing off!" Her voice was shrill and unrecognisable. "Don't you understand? Are you too bloody stupid to understand?"

"It's all right—everything is all right," Libby soothed and with a surprising show of strength half-lifted Silvia clear of the floor and bore her away into the main part of the house. It seemed to Dallen that Silvia's eyes again sought out his before two other women rallied to Libby's aid, closing in on Silvia and shutting her off from his view. He stared after them until a large petal of glass belatedly detached itself from the gutted screen and crashed to the floor. The sound of it triggered a crossfire of conversation in the group of watchers.

"Spectacular, wasn't it?" Renard murmured to Dallen. "Electra herself couldn't have put on a better show."

Dallen, baffled by the reference, saw that Renard was cool and untouched, perhaps even amused by the monumental act of destruction he had witnessed. "Rick, you're a real credit to the human race."

"What are you trying to say, old son?"

"That I don't like you and I'm getting dangerously close to doing something about it."

Renard looked gratified. "Which one of us do you reckon it's dangerous for?"

"Have a good trip to Orbitsville." Dallen turned to walk away and almost blundered into Peter Ezzati, who had removed his armband and was still looking flustered.

"Everything is happening at once," Ezzati said.

"Karal dying . . . the experiment . . . Silvia . . . And I was late getting here because I was following the news about Orbitsville. These green lights have to *mean* something, Garry. I'm starting to get a bad feeling about them."

"What green lights?" Dallen felt he had reached saturation point as far as new information was concerned, but something in Ezzati's manner prompted him to make the enquiry.

"Haven't you been following the news? They've discovered these bands of green light drifting across the shell, inside and out. At first they thought there was only going to be one, but more and more of them are showing up, getting closer together."

"Is it some kind of ionisation effect? Something like an aurora?"

Ezzati shook his head. "The Science Commission says the bands don't register on any type of detector they've got, except photographically. You can see them if you're looking directly at the shell, but that's all."

"Then they can't amount to much."

"I wish I could shrug them off like that," Ezzati said, frowning. "I don't like what's happening, Garry—the shell material is supposed to be totally stable."

"It isn't going to explode, you know." As a native of Orbitsville, one who had flown millions of kilometres over its grasslands and mountains and seas, Dallen clearly understood the sheer immutability of the vast globe. Since coming to Earth he had found that people who had never been to Orbitsville were unable to cope with its scale, and tended to think of it as something like a large metal balloon. The inadequacy of their vision was often shown in the way they spoke of people living *in* Orbitsville, whereas those who had first-hand experience invariably said *on* Orbitsville.

There could be no substitute for seeing the reality of the sphere from the direct observation area of a ship. Once was always enough. The Big O was daunting but somehow reassuring, and nobody who had ever looked on it could be quite the same person again.

"I'm not suggesting it's going to explode, it's just that . . ." Ezzati paused and cocked his head like a bird.

"I *knew* there was something else I had to tell you. With not coming into the office these days, I don't suppose you'll have heard about Gerald Mathieu."

"Mathieu?" Dallen held his voice steady. "What about him?"

"He set out for the west coast this morning, but he didn't get very far—his ship went down somewhere near Montgomery."

"Forced landing?"

"*Very* forced. From the analysis of the way his beacons snuffed out it looks as though he flew smack into a hill."

The words impacted on Dallen's mind like a bowling ball hurled with pin-splintering force, scattering all his preconceptions about the immediate future. Instead of satisfaction at the idea of Mathieu meeting a violent death, he felt an immediate sense of loss. It had to be wrong for the man who had casually destroyed a family to escape so easily, so quickly, without even knowing that he had been judged and condemned, without even looking into his executioner's eyes.

"Is there any definite . . .?" Dallen swallowed to ease the dryness in his throat. "Is Mathieu dead?"

"Don't let Silvia hear you use that word around here." Ezzati smiled broadly and patted Dallen's upper arm. "Discarnate is the accepted term. It looks as though young Mathieu is as discarnate as a dodo."

"I find that . . . hard to believe," Dallen said, belatedly coming to terms with the new situation. Mathieu's death had relieved him of a terrible responsibility, freeing him to deal with other commitments which, thus far, he had avoided thinking about in detail.

Ezzati looked up at him with some anxiety. "Look, Garry, I didn't mean to sound flippant. Was Mathieu close to you?"

"Not really. I'm going home." Dallen was outside the house and walking to his car, the world around him a blur of shimmering colours and steamy warmth, before he realised that he really was going home. He and Cona and Mikel had wasted too much time on Earth.

Chapter 13

The universe consisted of a bowl of pure blue glass.

Three objects had been tossed into the bowl and were lying, quite near each other, at the bottom of the azure curvature. Most prominent was a circular object which was intensely bright, so much so that it was painful to look directly at it. He classified it as a nearby sun. Next was a small, pale crescent, almost lost in the bombardment of light, and that had to be a non-radiant body—a planet or a moon.

The third object differed from the others in that it was larger and did not have precise geometries. It was a misty and elongated patch of white, with traces of a feathery internal structure. After some thought he identified it as a cloud.

The word initiated a rapid sequence of associations—atmosphere . . . moisture . . . rain . . . land . . . vegetation . . .

I'm alive!

The astonishing thought brought Mathieu to his feet in a split second, gasping with shock. He made several little darting runs in different directions, like a wild creature which had been trapped, only coming to a standstill when he realised the terrors were all in his mind, that no final calamity was about to overtake him. Nothing more could happen. He shaded his eyes and took his first near-rational look at the sunlit hillside.

Crimson and gold tatters of his aircraft were strewn over a wide area, and far off to his right the power plant was sending up plumes of smoke as it tried to ignite the lush grass. The pointed nose, minus its canopy, was the largest fuselage section to have survived the impact. A short distance behind the cockpit it had the semblance of a mashed cigar, ragged pennants of alloy skin enclosing a profusion of spar stumps, broken pipes and cables. Much farther down the slope was a surprisingly neat scar in the earth, as though some giant plough had upturned a short straight furrow.

Mathieu gave a shaky laugh which faded quickly into the surrounding stillness. To his own ears it had sounded insane. He examined himself and found that his tan suit was torn in places and was liberally smeared with soil and grass. A pulsing stiffness in his limbs told him he was extensively bruised, that in a day or two he would scarcely be able to move, but otherwise he was miraculously unharmed. A sudden weakness, engendered by awe rather than anything physical, caused him to sink to his knees.

I'm supposed to be dead!

The realisation that he had tried to commit suicide astonished Mathieu almost as much as his survival of the crash. He could think of nothing more stupid and pointless than ending his life, especially as the future had so much to offer. The only explanation he could suggest for his still being alive was that he had regained his sanity in the last hurtling seconds and had hauled back on the control column just in time—but what had prompted him to try killing himself in the first place?

A picture of Garry Dallen ghosted through Mathieu's consciousness—a swarthy Nemesis, hard-muscled, running in tireless pursuit, the handsome face cold and unforgiving, the eyes murderous . . .

Could that have been the reason? Fear of Garry Dallen, coupled with his own nagging remorse over what he had done to Dallen's wife and child?

Mathieu considered the matter carefully and felt his bafflement increase. Surely, no matter how much nervous stress he had been under, he would have needed better motives than those for committing suicide. He had nothing to fear from Dallen—for the straightforward reason that Dallen had no way to connect him with what had happened to his family. Mathieu had been very careful all along to cover his traces, to make sure that nobody in authority could find out about his private disposal of Metagov property. That had been the whole point in his blanking out of the Department of Supply monitor, and with its memory successfully obliterated he was doubly safe.

True, there had been the incident with Cona Dallen and her baby on the north stair, but Dallen had no way to link him with that, and it had not been premeditated. Sheer back luck had brought all three of them together at that crucial moment, and he had done only what he had to do to protect himself, no more and no less. It was regrettable that two other people had become involved in that way, but it was not as if he had committed murder. Two new personalities would emerge to replace those which had been lost—so, in a way, the books were balanced. Certainly, there was no reason for him to go through life burdened with remorse or guilt.

If anybody was to blame it was the crooked chemists and their dealers who charged such iniquitous prices for minute quantities of . . .

Mathieu stood up, plunged a hand into his inner pocket and withdrew his gold pen. It was undamaged. He clicked the barrel into the special position, priming it to dispense its magical ink, then paused and frowned down at the sunglittering cylinder. Upheavals were taking place within him; mental landscapes were undergoing cataclysmic change.

In a single movement he snapped the pen in half and hurled it away from him. He turned so that he was unable to note where the pieces fell and considered what he had just done, half-expecting an onslaught of panic. Instead he felt a sweet emptiness, a total lack of concern.

"Maybe I *am* dead," he said aloud, shaking his head in wonderment over the knowledge—so different from the vagrant hopes of the past—that he would never again have to use felicitin. So novel was the state of mind that it took him an appreciable time to interpret it, but he was no longer a user!

The feeling of certainty persisted even when he reviewed the medical facts. There was a distinct personality profile common to those who became dependent on the drug, and he had never heard of spontaneous remissions or unaided escapes. His entire future had been predicted around the fact that he was hooked on felicitin . . . (Was "hooked" a sufficiently graphic word? How about skewered? Or impaled?) . . . and now, suddenly, the drug was irrelevant.

A sputtering sound from the aircraft's power plant drew Mathieu's attention to the scattered wreckage, and his sense of wonder over his survival returned. The contours of the ground must have exactly matched the ship's line of flight, giving it seconds instead of microseconds in which to shed its kinetic energy, and thereby saving his life. Such events were not unknown in aviation lore—a similar thing had happened to St. Exupery in North Africa—but still he had a distinct sense of the miraculous. A religious man would have been down on his knees giving thanks to God. Mathieu, however, had more earthly concerns, among them the question of how long it would take him to get back to Madison City so that he could proceed with the important business of being alive.

He was alone in a sea of verdant green which shaded into blue as it reached the vaporous blur of the horizon. This area of what had once been Alabama had been deregistered more than a century earlier and now it looked as though it had never been touched, as though the first boats had yet to come straggling across the Pacific.

The nearest population centre was probably Madison City itself, hundreds of kilometres to the east, so there was no point in straying from the wreckage of his aircraft. With the gradual emptying of the country's airspace, all the paraphernalia of traffic control had been abandoned in favour of a system using computers in each aircraft. The transport department computer in Madison would have known about the crash as soon as it had happened, and in theory an emergency team should already be on its way to him.

Deciding that he should get some gentle exercise while waiting to be picked up, Mathieu began walking along the hillside. He had taken only a few paces when his attention was caught by a pulsing speck of ruby light which appeared low above the eastern horizon. It was the beacon of an aircraft which seemed to be heading in his direction.

He watched the approaching flier for a minute or more before realising it was a rescue ship.

The discovery was yet another shock in what seemed to be an endless series. He had assumed, in view of his sense of relative well-being, that he had been only lightly stunned in the crash—but the arrival of the recovery craft implied that he had been unconscious for a considerable time, perhaps as much as thirty minutes. In that case, according to his admittedly sketchy medical knowledge, he should have been suffering an intense headache and nausea. He prodded in a gingerly fashion around his skull, almost expecting to find a severe but previously unnoticed wound, and confirmed that he was basically uninjured.

The thunderous arrival of the high-speed ship cut short his speculations. It swooped down out of the sky, chunky fuselage bristling with cranes and other recovery gear, came to a halt at a height of some fifty metres and made a vertical descent on screaming reaction tubes. Grass blasted outwards from the touch-down point before the engines died, then a hatch in the ship's belly slid open. Four men, one of them carrying a stretcher, dropped out of it and came running towards Mathieu.

He gave an oddly self-conscious wave and walked to meet them, repressing the urge to chuckle as he got his first glimpse of their pop-eyed, slack-jawed expressions of pure astonishment.

The brandy was the first he had tasted in months, and Mathieu found it unusually satisfying. He took sip after sip of the neat liquor, relishing its warmth and flavour while he watched the countryside drift by beneath the rescue ship.

Even after they had checked him out with hand-held body scanners, confirming that he had no internal injuries, the medics had wanted to put him in a bunk for the return trip to Madison. Eventually, however, he had got his way and had been allowed to occupy a passenger seat in lordly isolation at the rear of the cabin. The medics and salvage experts were clustered at the front, and the frequency with which they glanced in his direction was a sign they had not from the shock of finding him in the land of the living.

Aided by the relaxing effect of the brandy, he amused himself by picturing how they would have taken the news of the second miracle, the private one. Almost a full hour had passed since he regained consciousness on the hillside, but there had been no wavering in his new attitude towards felicitin. He *knew* he was free of the addiction which had so grotesquely distorted his life, and now anything seemed possible . . .

The door to the flight deck slid open and a crewman came aft carrying a radiophone. He handed it to Mathieu, told him that Mayor Bryceland was calling and returned to his station. Bryceland was already speaking when Mathieu raised the instrument to his ear.

". . . only thing that matters is that you are all right, Gerald. That goes without saying. It's a big relief to all of us that you haven't been injured. My God, I mean . . . When I heard the ship had been *wrecked*!"

"You heard right, Frank," Mathieu said peacefully, having divined the real purpose of the call. "The ship doesn't exist any more."

"But if you're only bruised . . ."

"I was very lucky, Frank—I'm all right, but the ship is metal confetti." Mathieu paused, visualising the consternation on the mayor's puffy features, and decided to turn the screw a little more. "I'm glad things didn't work out the other way round."

"So am I—that goes without saying. I don't want to rush things, Gerald, but the insurance department boys have been at me already . . . Was there a control failure?"

"No. I fell asleep."

"Then the autopilot must have failed."

"I'd switched it off."

"Oh!" There was another pause and when Bryceland spoke again a noticeable coldness had appeared in his voice. "That wasn't too bright, was it?"

"It was pretty damn stupid. Suicidal, in fact."

Bryceland gave an audible sigh. "Gerald, you sound as if you're enjoying this."

"I am." Mathieu took a sip of brandy. "I'm going into orbit on free booze and laughing my head off over the entire episode."

"I'm going to assume it's shock that's making you talk this way."

"Not shock—it's the thought of you having to hoof

it like an ordinary mortal for a while. That's making me hysterical, Frank."

"I see," Bryceland said grimly. "Well, possibly by the time you get back into the office I'll have some news about your employment status that'll calm you down a bit."

"What makes you think I'll ever go back?" Mathieu broke the connection and set the phone down, aware that he had virtually thrown away his job. He took stock of his feelings and found no regrets. Until a short time ago the prospect of being fired would have terrified him, but now he was quite unmoved. It was, he realised, another consequence of his conversion. He no longer needed the job and all its opportunities for graft because he no longer needed felicitin. But what if, as had happened before, his lack of interest in the drug proved to be only temporary? What if it was all part of some complex response to the brush with death? One which would fade in a few hours?

The questions were pertinent, and there was an instant during which his system tried to react with panic, but the moment passed. It was as if the striker on an alarm bell had stirred briefly and then had returned to quiescence. His inner certainty prevailed, and now something new was being added.

There's nothing to keep me here on Earth, Mathieu thought. *And I'm no longer afraid of going to Orbitsville.*

The idea of returning to the place of his birth was strange, perhaps the most disturbing so far in the day's train of inner changes, and yet it was powerfully seductive. There was a felicitin-type *rightness* about it. His life on Earth had been a reenactment in miniature of the planet's own history. It had been a story

of waste, failure and futility, one which deserved to
be brought to a quick ending.

And it might be that the journey to Optima Thule
would be for him what it had been to the human race
in general—a rebirth, a radical change of direction, a
turning away from darkness and towards light.

The decision was instantaneous.

Mathieu set his glass aside, no longer interested in
its contents. He was going to Orbitsville and wanted
his departure to take place without delay, but there
were some practical problems. The sensible course
would be to patch up his relationship with Mayor
Bryceland, resign gracefully with the customary three
months' notice, and eventually leave for Orbitsville
with a fat severance payment logged into his bank
account. But to one in his frame of mind that approach seemed intolerably slow. His new impetuos-
ity told him he had done with Earth and therefore
should leave at once, which meant cutting a few
corners.

He leaned back in his chair, staring unseeingly at
the drifting landscape below, and analysed the problems facing him. Ships were travelling from Earth to
Ultima Thule every day, and with the tourist trade
in decline there was no shortage of passenger places,
but Mathieu's difficulties lay elsewhere. He had only
a small reserve of cash, and walking out on his job
was going to deprive him of some benefits and cause
long delays with others—all of which meant he would
be hard pressed to cover the cost of an unsubsidised
ticket. There was an additional complication in the
form of Mayor Bryceland, who would not want him
to leave before a replacement arrived, and therefore

would do everything in his power to block the clear-ances necessary for travel on a Metagov-owned ship.

What Mathieu needed was somebody who con-trolled the physical means of getting to Orbitsville and who also owed him a favour. Years of constantly being on the make had led him to build up a range of useful contacts, many of them of a somewhat irregu-lar nature, but privately owned or chartered starships were something of a rarity. There *was* somebody, though—it was simply the matter of locating the right file in his memory—and that somebody was . . .

Mathieu gave a self-satisfied grunt when a name formed itself in his thoughts almost at once. Rick Renard, the playboy botanist, was reputed to have connections with the legendary Lindstrom family, and for that reason Mathieu had been exceptionally helpful to him. The indulgences had ranged from overlooking a sheaf of import restrictions on a fancy Rollac car to allowing publicly owned warehouses to be used for the temporary storage of botanical samples. And, providentially it seemed, Renard was soon to depart for Orbitsville.

I've found the way, Mathieu thought, reaching for the radiophone, unable to delay taking immediate and positive action. *I'm going home at last.*

Chapter 14

It was not until his car had struck the curb for the second time that Dallen realised how the sheer mental overload of the past hour had rendered him unfit to drive.

He braked and pulled in to the side in one of the North Hill's quietest avenues. The car shuddered slightly as he switched off the engine. He located his pipe in a jacket pocket, filled it with strands of yellow and black, abstractedly staring straight ahead as he tamped them down with his finger. It seemed that each time he visited the London place he got his consciousness stretched, but the last occasion had left him with no reserve capacity whatsoever. So many new matters clamoured and competed for his consideration that he was unable to focus properly on any of them.

Impose some order, he told himself. *Find patterns*.

The task struck him as being impossible, and the most he could do, sitting in the metal-and-glass suntrap of his car, was to pick out certain symmetries.

Karal London was dead—but Karal London could not be dead, only made discarnate. The success of his fantastic experiment had profound significance for religion and philosophy, and yet as far as emotions were concerned it seemed to have little immediate relevance. Silvia's reaction had shown that. Death continued to be Death, no matter what the cool voice of the intellect proclaimed; and men and women would still mourn its intervention just as they had always done. The racial subconscious would have to assimilate a great deal of mindon science before there dawned the era of the blithe burial or the cheerful cremation, before London was hailed as the man who put the fun into funeral.

Gerald Mathieu was dead—but Gerald Mathieu could not be dead, only made discarnate. What was the personal significance of that for Dallen? The wash of photons from a single light bulb in London's laboratory had carried the message that Mathieu, too, had entered an afterlife and would exist perhaps for ever as a mindon entity. Did that mean the whole concept of punishment by execution was now invalid? Perhaps the only genuine retribution would have lain in making the punishment fit the crime, in blasting Mathieu's physical brain with a Luddite Special and scattering its mindon counterpart to whatever kind of thin winds that blew through an extra-dimensional ether. And now it was too late even to think about that.

In any case, the dominating element of revenge had been removed from Dallen's life, and the resultant vacuum had been filled by new emotions centred on Silvia London. Silvia was going to Orbitsville, and—further symmetry—so was he . . .

Feeling the mental convection begin again, the restless whirlwind of thought fragments, he seized on the prospect of leaving for the Big O. That was a concrete fact, one which involved him in practical matters and a host of auxilliary decisions. He could, for instance, go immediately to the City Hall, arrange a transfer to Orbitsville on the next scheduled flight and clear out his desk. A good clear-cut short-term goal. A way to deaden his mind and at the same time delay the moment when he would have to return home and pick up the burden represented by Cona.

The decision made, Dallen discovered he had forgotten to light his pipe. He dropped it back into his pocket, switched on the car's magnetic engine and drove down the Hill towards the centre of Madison. Bars of tree-shadow and sunlight beat silently on the vehicle in quickening tempo. Traffic was quite sparse at that time of the afternoon and it took him less than ten minutes to reach the City Hall and park near the main entrance.

He went straight to his office on the second floor and paused when he saw the unfamiliar name plate on the door. It said: M.K.L.BYROM. Dallen had forgotten that his post was being filled by a replacement Grade IV officer who had been flown down from Winnipeg. He tapped the door, walked into the office without waiting for an invitation and was surprised to find Jim Mellor, his senior deputy, who usually worked in the operations centre, seated alone at the big communications console.

"Garry!" Mellor grinned, hoisting his tall crane-like figure out of the chair, and shook Dallen's hand. "What are you doing here?"

"I should be asking you that. Promotion?"

"No chance! I came over to mind the shop for a while."

"Well, I only came in to notify somebody that I'm quitting this job and transferring back home on the first available ship. Consider yourself notified."

"I guessed you'd be doing that sooner or later, but you ought to give the word to Ken Byrom."

"I've no more time for all the red tape. Why can't you pass the good news on on my behalf?"

"You know, Garry—proper channels. Besides, he wants to have a few words with you."

"What about?"

"Ken likes everything done according to directives. He's all knotted up over the weapon you lost in Cordele—not to mention taking a ship while you were officially on leave."

"Tell him to . . ." Dallen studied the other man's narrow face. "Did you drop yourself in it by tipping me off about Beaumont?"

"Me!" Mellor looked indignant. "I never tipped nobody off, not noways nohow."

"You're one of the people I'm going to miss around here," Dallen said, briefly gripping one of Mellor's stringy biceps. "Now, I'm going to collect a few things from my desk and . . ."

"Ken has done all that for you." Mellor opened a closet, took out a large bulging envelope and handed it to Dallen. "I think he wants a permanent assignment in Madison."

"He's welcome. Why isn't he here, anyway?"

"Went across to the inner field with a bunch of the others to see Gerald Mathieu."

"Mathieu?" The tone and content of what he had just heard flicked at Dallen's nerves.

"Yeah. You know about what happened to him?"

"I heard."

"Wildest thing! That's why this place is empty—they all had to have a look for themselves."

Dallen considered the first meaning that Mellor's words had for him—that a large group of normal people had flocked across town to view a plastic sack full of bloody tissue and bone splinters—and was forced to reject it. The alternative, the incredible alternative, was a chaotic new element in the agitation that already existed in his thoughts. Gerald Mathieu still alive! *Still alive!* Dallen abruptly felt sick and bruised, like a fighter on the ropes.

He pretended to check the contents of his envelope. "Lucky escape, was it?"

"Lucky!" Mellor flung up his arms in protest at the inadequacy of the word. "He went into a hill at one K! The ship was reduced to chaff, but Mathieu walked away from it with nothing worse than bruises. What a guy!"

"The cockpit must have been in one piece."

"Yeah, the *cockpit* must have been in one piece, but the rest of the ship . . . Hey, Garry, you don't have anything against Mathieu, do you?"

"Of course not. Why do you ask?"

"Nothing. It was just the way you . . ."

"I'll see you around, Jim." Dallen left the office and stood for a moment in the cottony silence of the corridor, trying to reorganise his thoughts. Everything had changed once again. It was a perfect illustration of the intense relationship that binds a hunter to his quarry, forcing him to follow every swing and swerve with greater and greater concentration and fidelity until the pursuit reaches its climax. His life would not be his own again until Mathieu was dead, and that—much though he disliked the idea—meant delaying the return of the Dallen family to Orbitsville.

The first sensible step in the new situation should be to withdraw his verbal resignation, but he was in no mood to face Mellor again at that moment. Mellor was not a particularly perceptive man, but he had picked up Dallen's resentment over hearing Mathieu spoken with admiration. That had been a lapse on Dallen's part, and it was something he would have to take extra care over if—as was quite possible, given the irrationality of most human beings—Mathieu were to be elevated to the status of local hero because of his amazing luck. It was important for Dallen to show no enmity towards Mathieu, to display no special interest. On the other hand, he should display no special *lack* of interest either . . . Or was his thinking becoming too involuted and obsessional?

Frowning, breathing deeply to ease the growing pressure between his temples, Dallen walked along the corridor towards the elevator which would drop him into the building's main reception area. In the past he would have taken a short cut by way of the north-side emergency stair, but that was a trick he had passed on to Cona, and as a result of it she and Mikel had been . . . He wrenched his thoughts back into the present as a door opened just ahead of him. Vik Costain, personal assistant to the Mayor, came hurrying through it and almost collided with Dallen.

"I'm *so* sorry," Costain exclaimed in his prissy manner. There was a flustered expression on his grey face and his hairless scalp was glistening with perspiration.

"You should slow down a bit," Dallen said, "or get personal radar."

"Spare me the witticisms, Garry—this has been the worst afternoon in my thirty years in this place."

"Frank giving you a hard time?"

Costain turned his eyes up for a second. "Between him and Beau bloody Brummel . . ."

"Who?"

"Young Mathieu. They've been having a radio-phone battle for the last hour and I'm right in the middle of it, and there's nobody here to do any goddamn *work*. I suppose you've heard the latest about Mathieu?"

Dallen nodded. "Mister Indestructible."

"Not that," Costain said impatiently. "He has just quit his job without giving notice, and that throws his workload on to Frank and me. Frank is furious."

"I'll bet he is," Dallen said, again the hunter, feeling the hunter's quickening of the pulse as the trail makes a sudden swing. "What is Gerald planning to do with himself?"

"Orbitsville. He claims he's getting out immediately on some kind of special flight. Have you ever heard of this Renard character?"

"Renard?" Dallen felt a sick satisfaction, a furtive and intoxicating glee, which spread through him as he imagined being close to Mathieu for almost a week in the unnatural environment of a starship. So many dangerous complexities, so many traps for the unwary, so many ways in which a man could be overtaken by premature death . . .

"As a matter of fact," he said peacefully, "Rick Renard and I are good friends. Oddly enough, I've been thinking of going home with him on the same flight."

Chapter 15

Renard's ship detached itself from Polar Band One and began the long climb to the edge of interstellar space.

Almost half-a-century old, the *Hawkshead* was a bulk cargo freighter which had been built when Earth's space technology was still high on a crest. It had the classic configuration developed by the historic Starflight company—three equal cylinders joined together in parallel, with the central one projecting ahead by almost half its length. The control deck, living quarters and cargo space were in the central cylinder; the outer pair housing the thermonuclear drivers and flux pumps, plus the warp generators which were only brought into play in the higher speed regimes. Because the huge magnetic fields created by the pumps swirled out symmetrically from the fuselage, ships of the type were popularly known as flickerwings, though the name was misleading. The fields were vast insubstantial scoops which gathered interstellar matter for use as reaction mass.

Spatial weather conditions were good as the *Hawks-head* spiralled outwards from the orbit of Earth. Great billows of energetic particles which had originated in the heart of the galaxy were rolling across the Solar System. These sprays of fast-moving corpuscles— which meant as much to the starship as wind, wave and tide had done to oceanic clippers—provided a rich harvest for the vessel's drivers, enabling it to accelerate at better than 1G.

In the first century of interstellar travel it had been necessary for a ship to attain a speed of some fifty million metres a second before it entered a paradoxical domain, governed by the laws of the Canadian mathematician Arthur Arthur, where Einsteinian ideas about space and time no longer held sway. Arthurian physics had made it possible for a ship to journey between Earth and Orbitsville in only four months, with almost no relativistic time dilation, but even that kind of mind-defying speed had been insufficient for the needs of the Migration. The solution, born out of experience and computer-enhanced genius, had been the tachyonic mode, described by one orthodox theorist as "crooked accountancy applied to mass-energy tranformations", and it had cut the transit time to an average of six days.

It was a brief time by anybody's standards, and that thought was much on Dallen's mind as he stood in the ship's observation gallery and watched the Earth-Moon system begin to shrink to the semblance of a double star. His move against Gerald Mathieu would have to be made very soon.

Dallen had been too busy winding up his affairs in Madison to think much about the journey which lay ahead, but in view of the circumstances he had half-expected some of the features of an old-style oceanic cruise. He had visualised Renard sitting at the head of the evening dinner table, with Silvia London nearby, revelling in and taking every conceivable social advantage from his position as benefactor-employer. That notion had been compounded from ignorance of conditions aboard freighters and the assumption that Renard would have despotic control over the ship's daily routine.

In actuality Renard seemed to spend most of his time in bitter argument with the freighter's captain, Lars Lessen, a morose, pigeon-chested man in his fifties. Lessen, it transpired, had undertaken to provide a crew and run the ship on a fixed-price contract, and he was deeply unhappy with the way things were working out.

Forty years earlier the *Hawkshead* would almost have flown itself to Orbitsville. Now more and more human interventions were required to keep its myriad systems in operation, and the extra man-hour payments were gnawing into Lessen's profits. He reacted by waging psychological warfare on Renard—one tactic being to call him with unnecessary frequency over minor decisions—and to Dallen's surprise seemed to be gaining the upper hand, evidence of the advantages of playing on one's home ground.

The ship had one largish canteen area, in place of Dallen's imagined dining room, but it was jealously monopolised by the thirty-strong crew. The group of ten supernumeraries recruited by Renard were more-or-less expected to use the mealomat dispensers and eat in their rooms. These were prefabricated cabins

ranged in a partial circle on Deck 5, the one just
above the vertiginous well of the cargo hold.

The living arrangements, which could have been
described as unsociable, came as an unwelcome surprise to the others, but they suited Dallen quite well
because Cona had not taken to space travel. She had
become hysterical during the brief shuttle ride to the
ship, necessitating heavy sedation, and had continued
to react badly to the confinement of the cabin Dallen
shared with her and Mikel. The only way he could
keep on top of the situation was by dosing her with a
tranquiliser prescribed by Roy Picciano, a drug which
on Dallen's insistence included an effective libido
depressant.

Mikel was rapidly becoming a normal-seeming
infant, one who played a lot with his toy vehicles and
showed an obvious pleasure on seeing his father, but
Dallen found himself still unable to make a whole-
hearted response. No matter how often he cursed
himself for the lack of emotional generosity there
remained a hint of reserve, a stubborn feeling that
fate was a salesman trying to fob him off with a
substitute product.

The story of what had happened to his family was
quick to circulate among the *Hawkshead*'s crew, bringing sympathy he could well have done without, but a
welcome result was that four women in the field
engineering section volunteered a baby-minding service.
Dallen accepted with gratitude, conscious of the fact
that no matter how much genuine concern other men
might show for one in his predicament it was always
women who came through with the sort of practical
help which made a difference in life's daily battles.
As well as freeing him to do his quota of work on the

grass trays, the arrangement gave Dallen some extra time with his fellow passengers.

The first shipboard meeting with Gerald Mathieu was a tableau of civilised awkwardness and non-communication. It took place on the narrow strip of deck between the cabins and the abyss of the ship's hold. There were no other people in sight, and as the two men drew together Dallen was almost swamped by a manic urge to seize his chance, to end his baleful and unnatural involvement with the other man in a single burst of primitive violence. For one thunderous instant the idea seemed almost feasible—a sudden grapple and lift, a body plunging into the lethal steel-spiked depths, a story about a freak accident . . .

But what sort of accident?

The guard rail was chest-high and, try as he might, Dallen was unable to invent an incident in which one man could be propelled to his death without suspected homicidal intent on the part of the other. Abruptly the crucial moment passed, its karma-potential fading. There was a sense of ponderous wheels, having hesitated, juddering into a new set of positions—and now Dallen was faced with the problem of how to address a person he saw only as a walking corpse.

"Hello, Gerald," he said, smiling, glancing at the spartan surroundings. "Like to buy a ticket for the mutiny?"

Mathieu met his gaze squarely. "That's yard-arm talk, Mister Christian."

Christian? Dallen thought, disconcerted. *I've got to start reading books, the way Cona wanted.*

Before he could compose a reply the odd little nonincident was over and the tall figure of Mathieu was moving out of sight between two cabins, ice-smooth blond hair glowing dully in the ship's dismal illumination. He was wearing immaculate silvery grey casuals—his idea of clothes suitable for manual work—and looked as composed and urbane as ever, but Dallen thought he had detected a difference in the man. Had it been in the hard calmness of the eyes? Was that typical of one who was stoking up on felicitin, or had Mathieu's skirmish with death—by all accounts a remarkable escape—wrought some profound change in his character?

It makes no difference, Dallen told himself, rejecting the alien idea which had tried to enter his mind, the idea that Mathieu was in the process of becoming a new person, one who might not deserve the fate which was in store for him. Dallen had little patience with any kind of violent criminal, but the species he had least time for were those who murdered innocents and then, while their appeals against execution were filtering through, composed books or holoplays about the sanctity of human life. He denied Mathieu any right to plead "not guilty for reasons of resurrection". It was essential that the issues of life and death, crime and punishment, sin and retribution should retain their old clairty—enough complication had already been introduced into his thoughts by the Karal London experiment.

Mathieu and London should have remained in separate compartments of his life, but they had a disconcerting way of merging in his thoughts like images in an antique stereo viewer, both of which had to contribute to make a rounded picture. London taught that after death there came new life. Mathieu had already enacted his own little pastiche on that theme—

the shock of his "death" and return to life was still reverberating in Dallen's system—and the philosophical implications continued to cloud his thinking about his family tragedy.

Given that there was no such thing as death in the former sense of the word, that it was merely the gateway to a new existence, could execution still be regarded as a penalty? What kind of punishment was it that simply advanced the next phase of an evildoer's life? And, going further, how serious a crime was murder if it meant that the victim had similarly been introduced to his own immortality?

It makes no difference, Dallen repeated to himself, angered by the mental clamour following his deceptively bland encounter with Mathieu. He returned to his own cabin and spent some time examining the contents of the small travel bag he had privately labelled his execution kit.

It held a miscellany of items ranging from blades and wires to drug containers, gathered almost at random, any of which might become an unobtrusive murder weapon in suitable circumstance. No plan had yet crystallised, but some dark instinct kept drawing his attention to the most innocent-seeming object of the lot—a miniature spraycan of paint he had taken from Madison City's transport workshops.

The first in-flight meeting with Silvia London was equally unsatisfactory from Dallen's viewpoint.

He had not seen her since her cathartic act of destroying the glass mosaic in her home, but he knew she was being accompanied on the journey by two officers of the Anima Mundi Foundation. Both were women and previously unknown to him. They had

dealt with the considerable media interest given to
Silvia before the start of the voyage, and now seemed
to be coaching her for various kinds of public appear-
ances in major cities. Their presence reminded Dallen
that Karal London, in spite of the obviously cranky
aspects of his operation, had been a determined and
far-sighted man with a serious mission in life. It also
made him wonder if he had allowed himself to be too
much influenced by Renard's male chauvinist analysis of Silvia's relationship with the dead man.

Her reaction to the news of London's "discarnation"
had, in a way, pleased him with its message that she
was far from being the simplistic sexual timebomb
described by Rick Renard—but there was another
part of him, repressed throughout his adult life, which
savoured the thought of being the first to bed a
voluptuous young woman after she had been de-
prived of sex for two years. And his emotional dichot-
omy was made worse by the fact that he was quite
unable to read Silvia's signals, had no way of knowing if what had passed between them meant everything or nothing. One interpretation was that he was
a fantastically lucky man who had only to reach out
his hand and take one of life's choicest offerings;
another was that he was an overgrown adolescent
with delusions inspired by a surplus of imagination,
conceit and hormones.

I fail to see the difficulty, old son, he could imagine
Renard saying to him, were he himself not one of the
problem's parameters. *Why not simply go ahead and try
your luck?*

Why not indeed? Dallen asked himself as he entered
the Deck 4 compartment which contained the bank of
mealomats and saw the black-clad figure of Silvia

amid a group of five women at the machines. Unfortunately the question presupposed his being a normal man in normal circumstances. There was no allowance for internal confusions and conflicts, for his unmanning guilt over Cona and Mikel, for his dehumanising compulsion to annihilate Gerald Mathieu, for his reluctance to resolve the question of Silvia too soon in case it transpired that it had all been a game which Renard had won in advance by virtue of his money, power and grinning confident insensitivity.

Silvia was discussing the choice of food with a companion, and as Dallen drew near he saw that, although slightly pale, she looked as though she had recovered from her period of trauma. He took in the firm-jawed face and the prominence of the lower lip, the massy fullness of breasts emphasised by the flatness of abdomen, the air of easy strength combined with femininity, and inside him was born a pain which had something to do with the fact that he had never read poetry and therefore did not have access to the words needed to let Silvia know how he felt about her. He was hesitating, overwhelmed, when she looked in his direction. She carried on her conversation without the slightest break, but her eyes engaged Dallen's and remained there, unwavering, while he moved towards another row of machines.

He smiled at her, then developed the conviction it was the same meaningless facial grimace he had made earlier on meeting Mathieu, and deliberately broke the visual contact by moving behind a drinks dispenser. Freed of the intense emotional pull, he selected food for Cona and himself, and when he emerged from an alley of cabinets Silvia was gone.

A few minutes later, back in his cabin, he found

Cona sitting on the edge of her bed, blinking drowsily
Her smock had ridden up to her broadening hips
exposing a wisp of colourless hair at the juncture o
puckered thighs. He twitched the hem of the gar
ment down to her knees and began setting out dishe
of food on the foldaway table. The air smelled o
stale perspiration.

"Din," Cona mouthed with effort. "Di-in."

"Very good," Dallen said, blanking out his freshly
renewed mental image of Silvia's face. "Say dinner
Din-*ner*."

"*Din*," Cona shouted in sudden manic joviality.
lurching towards the table. She picked up a spoon.
holding it sideways in her fist, and reached for a dish
of chocolate mousse. Dallen had found that if he gave
in and permitted her to eat some dessert at the beginning of a meal it was then quite easy to coax her into
having a fair amount of the main protein dish, but all
at once the idea was intolerable.

Without speaking, he closed his hand over Cona's
and steered the spoon towards a block of moulded
salad. She froze for a moment, then began to resist
with her considerable strength. Before he quite knew
what he was doing, he had half-risen to his feet to
gain leverage and had clamped Cona's head aginst his
hip. Subduing her with furious ease, he forced her to
take salad on to the spoon and was guiding it to her
mouth when something prompted him to glance towards a mirrored wall at the far side of the room.

The tableau he saw there, with its ancient formalised
compostion—oppressor looming over the oppressed—
could have been from any period in history. The
medium could have been grainy 20th Century or
age-darkened oil paint or perspectiveless woodcut,

but the principal elements were the same. Faces of torturer and victim alike—both robbed of all humanity— turned towards the camera-artist as though demanding to go on record for posterity. Dallen released his wife at once and stood facing his reflection.

"Bastard," he whispered. "The bastard has to pay."

Chapter 16

As a preliminary to the execution Dallen kept a close watch on Mathieu's movements.

He was quickly rewarded by the discovery that Mathieu, even when he had a freedom of choice, preferred a fixed pattern of activity. The work schedule called for each person in Renard's team to be responsible for two adjacent stacks of grass trays, the most tedious task being the rotation of the sunlight panels to give a reasonable simulation of night and day. Each tray also had to be lightly watered at some time during its "night" period. There was no hard-and-fast rule about exactly when the watering should be carried out, but Mathieu liked to do it as soon as he had removed each sunlight panel, starting at the top of the stacks and methodically working down to deck level.

Every morning at eleven, ship time, he climbed a twenty-metre alloy ladder attached to the front of one stack and serviced its top layer of trays. That done, he stretched all the way across the aisle and worked on his other stack from its rear, taking advantage of his long reach to avoid making two separate ascents. It was a technique of which Renard did not approve, but he had contented himself by sourly reminding Mathieu he was not covered by industrial insurance. And Dallen had listened to that particular exchange with satisfaction, knowing it would help smooth his way through what was to follow . . .

On the fifth morning of the voyage he awoke early. Cona was snoring peacefully in her bed at the other side of the prefab, and Mikel was fast asleep in his cot, one foot projecting through the bars. There was little in the peaceful tallowy dimness of the cabin to indicate that it was part of an engineered structure which was hurtling through distorted geometries of space. Were it not for near-subliminal, amniotic fluttering in the air Dallen could have believed himself to be in a holiday chalet anywhere on Earth or Orbitsville. His thoughts turned at once to Silvia London, only a few paces and partitions away on the same deck, but he hurriedly blanked out a vision of how she might look in bed. His morning erections were becoming painfully insistent, and on this crucial day all his mental and physical energies had to be directed elsewhere.

He quietly got out of bed and took stock of his emotions, trying to ascertain how he felt about his decision to proceed immediately with Mathieu's execution. There was a certain sense of disbelief mingled with a cold sadness and fears for his own safety— but the basic resolution was still there, intact, a dominating force which excluded compassion or regrets.

That's all right, he thought, unaccountably relieved. *Nothing has changed.*

Taking care not to disturb Cona or Mikel, he used the radiation shower cubicle—wishing it could have been a stinging water spray—and got dressed in the soft shirt and slacks which were his usual working attire. He brought the travel bag out of a closet and took from it the small container of special paint, which he put in his breast pocket.

There was nobody else abroad on Deck 5 when he left his cabin, so we went straight to the tubular elevator cage, dropped himself to the bottom of the cargo hold and stepped out into an angular jungle of scaffolding. Tall stacks of grass trays, half of them glowing under artificial sunlight, created a three-dimensional confusion of brilliance and shadow. There were puddles on the floor and the air was warm and humid, rich with meadow scents, dulling metal surfaces with condensation.

It took Dallen less than a minute to make sure no others had showed up early for work, then he went to Mathieu's two stacks and climbed the innermost ladder, the one always used by Mathieu. At the top, precisely when it was necessary for him to be alert and at peak efficiency, he was numbed by an awareness that he was at the point of maximum danger. He was only a few metres below the ring-shaped Deck 5, in a position readily visible to anyone who might emerge from a passenger cabin, and now his scheme—so foolproof when evaluated in the security of his bed—seemed reckless beyond belief.

With a final swinging glance at the circular guard rail above, he took the paint container out of his shirt pocket and sprayed a colourless fluid on to the ladder's top rung. Highly nervous, fighting off a tendency to shake, he returned the container to his pocket and slid commando-fashion to the foot of the ladder. The greenhouse stillness of the bottom deck was heavy and undisturbed. Dallen ran to the elevator, took it up to Deck 5 and within a matter of seconds was back in the sanctuary of his cabin, where Cona and Mikel were still asleep. The entire sortie had taken approximately three minutes.

Dallen sat down at the table and considered what he had done. The emulsion with which he had sprayed the ladder was manufactured for law enforcement bodies under the brand name of Pietzoff, and it was peculiarly suitable for his purpose. It was used to prevent people clinging to security vehicles and the vulnerable wing generator tubes of aircraft. Finger pressure on the deposited crystals would produce a neural shock which would affect Mathieu's whole body, not only repelling him from the ladder but preventing him from grasping anything which might lessen his fall.

There was no absolute guarantee that the impact with deck would kill him, but Dallen intended to be close to the scene of the "accident", first to reach the fallen man, and would need only the briefest moment to complete his work. An extra shearing of the neck vertebrae would go unnoticed among Mathieu's other injuries. The final step would be to ascend the ladder, ostensibly checking for faults, and wipe away the Pietzoff emulsion with the solvent sponge already in his pocket.

At that point, justice having been done, he could return to a normal life.

Dallen spread his hands on the table and frowned down at them as—for the first time—he tried to envisage the future which lay beyond Mathieu's death. What would constitute a "normal" life in his case? A Metagov job sufficiently undemanding that he would be able to devote most of his time to rehabilitating Cona? Perhaps he would be provided with a pension on compassionate grounds and given a house on the edge of one of those heroic developments which straggled a short distance into Orbitsville's endless oceans of grass. That way he could make Cona his life's work—and what would the career landmarks be? The day she learned to flush the toilet for herself? The day she completed her first sentence? The first night on which, in the mental chaos of the dark hours, he failed to turn her away from his bed?

Abruptly Dallen felt that he was drowning. He dismissed the feeling as a psychological effect, then realised he had breathed out and had actually omitted to initiate the next inhalation, as though his autonomous nervous system had gone on strike. He snatched air in two noisy sighs and sprang to his feet, feeling trapped within the confines of the cabin. The time display on the wall showed that it was not yet eight in the morning. Food? Would breakfast help? Dallen felt his diaphragm heave gently at the thought of eating, but coffee seemed a reasonably inviting prospect, a way of getting through a few minutes.

He made sure that Cona and Mikel were not likely to awaken, let himself out of the cabin and went upstairs to Deck 4, the first full deck. There was nobody in the mealomat area, although he could hear some crew members talking in the adjoining canteen.

Dallen drew himself a cup of black coffee, considered taking it into the canteen, then on impulse walked up another flight of stairs and went into the small observation gallery. It was deserted. Such vantage points tended to be used only during normal-space manoeuvring in the vicinity of Earth or Orbitsville—in mid-voyage, cocooned in a ship's private continuum, there was little to see outside. The universe presented itself as an intense spot of blue ahead of the ship and an equally bright locus of red astern. On the rare occasions when a vessel passed close to a star an ultra-thin ring of light would expand out of the forward spot, slide by the ship on all sides like a conjurer's hoop and shrink into the speck of ruby brilliance behind.

Unconcerned about the lack of spectacle, Dallen dropped into a chair and sat in the theatrical darkness sipping his coffee, his thoughts still dominated by the future. Fixing the time of Mathieu's execution seemed to have removed a short-term goal which had acted as a barrier. Now the shutters had been lifted and decades lay ahead of him in a blur of shifting probabilities—and from what he could see of the temporal landscape it looked bleak. To be more analytical, without Silvia London it looked bleak. To be even more analytical—and to add a dash of honesty and self-interest—*with* Cona and *without* Silvia it looked bleak.

And that, came the insidious thought, *is a circumstance that can easily be changed.*

All he had to do was quit being stubborn and accept what qualified physicians had been telling him all along—that Cona Dallen, author and historian, no

longer existed. That meant he had no moral obliga-
tions to her, that all contracts were nullified. The
body Cona had inhabited was entitled to good care,
to the comfort and security in which a new personality would be able to develop within its own limitations,
but there was no logical reason for Garry Dallen's
own life to be subordinated to the process. He should
be concerned, but not interned. He had placed himself in a prison whose walls were made of mist, and
all he had to do was walk free . . .

Fine! QED! Welcome to the bright, shadow-free world
of rationality!

Dallen felt a surge of elation and wonderment over
how easy it had been to put his life into logical order,
a sense of giddy uplift which was immediately followed by the plunging realisation that he had achieved
precisely nothing. He was building castles of romantic dreams around Silvia London—all on the strength
of a few ambiguous words and enigmatic looks. What
he needed was hard information, a straight yes or no
from the woman in question, but right from the
beginning he had behaved like a tongue-tied yokel in
Silvia's presence . . .

"In the name of *Christ*!" he whispered savagely,
swept by a sudden boiling surf of impatience over a
state of mind in which he could calmly arrange the
death of a fellow human being and at the same time
cower back from asking one question of a woman.
He crushed the empty cup in his right hand, producing a loud crackle which caused a barely-seen figure
to glance in his direction from the opposite end of
the gallery. The other person was a woman, and he
had no idea how long she had been sitting there. He

identified the thick-set, middle-aged figure as Doctor Billy Glaister, the Foundation officer who shared a cabin with Silvia, and he found himself moving towards her with no conscious sense of volition. She looked up in surprise, her face an indistinct glow in the darkness, as he halted at her side.

"Hello," Dallen said. "Restful in here, isn't it?"

"Usually," she replied coolly. "I come here when I want peace to think."

"Hint taken." Dallen tried an ingratiating chuckle. "I'll clear off and leave you to it. By the way, is Silvia in her room?"

"I expect so. Why?" The doctor had ceased being distant and now was openly hostile.

The notion that here might be another rival for Silvia immediately appeared in Dallen's mind, but something—all the more momentous for being unanticipated—had happened inside him and he welcomed the extra challenge. He hunkered down beside the woman, deliberately invading her personal space.

"I want to have a word with her. I presume she's allowed visitors?"

"Don't be impertinent. Silvia has had many stressful factors to contend with lately."

"It was decent of you to step out and give her a break." Dallen stood up, left the observation gallery and walked quickly towards the nearest stair.

The time was 8:50, leaving him more than two hours before his preordained rendezvous, and he felt a vast relief over the knowledge that he was at last committed to positive action. He was alert and competent, as though he had shaken off an enervating spell. He descended to Deck 5 and, not sparing a

glance for the netherworld of scaffolding and lights
visible in the central well, went to the box-like cabin
being used by Silvia and tapped the door. She opened
it, immediately spung away from him with a swirl of
a blue cotton dressing gown, then froze in mid-stride
and turned back.

"I thought you were . . ." Her eyes were wide with
surprise, seeming darker than usual against a morning paleness he had never seen before and which gave
him a stabbing sexual thrill of such power that he
almost gasped.

"May I come in?" he said steadily.

Silvia shook her head. "It's too . . . I'm not even
dressed."

"I've got to come in." He crossed the threshold and
closed the door. "I have to talk to you."

"About what?"

"No more games, Silvia. I know I shouldered my
way in here uninvited. I know I'm being bad-mannered
and that my timing couldn't be worse, but I have to
know about us. I need a direct statement from you—a
simple yes or a simple no."

"You make it seem like a business transaction."
Silvia appeared to have recovered her composure, but
her colour had heightened.

"Is this better?" He took the single pace that was
necessary to close the distance between them and,
very slowly, allowing her ample time to twist away,
placed a hand at each side of her waist and gently
drew her towards him. She came to him, yielding
with a peculiar sagging movement which brought
their groins together first—sending a shockwave of
sensation racing through his body—followed by a

leisurely meeting of bellies, breasts and mouths. Dallen drank the kiss, gorging himself until its natural ending.

"I've still got to hear you say it," he whispered, touching his lips to her ear. "Yes or no?"

"This isn't fair."

"To hell with fair—I've had enough fairness to last me a lifetime. Yes or no?"

"Yes." She thrust herself against him almost aggressively, with a force he had difficulty in matching. "*Yes!*"

"That's all I need to know." Intensely aware that the dressing gown was no longer fully lapped around her torso, he closed his eyes to kiss Silvia again and found himself looking at Gerald Mathieu's broken corpse.

"Trouble is," he said, floundering and distracted, "I'm not sure what to do next."

She smiled calmly. "How about locking the door?"

"Good thinking." Dallen thumbed the door's security button and when he turned back to Silvia the dressing gown was around her ankles on the floor. Dry-mouthed and reverent, he surveyed her body, then took her extended hand and went with her to the bed. She lay down at once and locked herself on to him, now trembling, as he positioned himself beside her. They clung together for a full minute, he still clothed, simulating the sex act in a way which by every law of nature should have aroused him to near-orgasm, but each time he allowed his eyes to close there was Mathieu's serene-smiling death mask with the tridents of blood at each corner of the mouth and the anaesthetic coldness was gathering in his own loins, emasculating him, denying him any stake in the game of Life. Without waiting for Silvia to sense what was happening, he rolled away from her and dropped into a kneeling posture at the side of the bed. She raised herself on one elbow and looked at him in puzzled reproach.

"It's all right," he said, almost grinning with relief at the clarity of his understanding of the situation. "This won't make any sense to you, Silvia, but I was trying to be two people at once, and it can't work."

"That makes perfectly good sense to me." Her understanding was intuitive, almost telepathic. "How long will it take you to become one people?"

Dallen gazed at her in purest gratitude. "About two minutes. There's something I have to do. Would you please wait? Right here? Like this?"

"I wasn't planning to go anywhere."

"Right." He stood up, strode to the door of the cabin and let himself out. *A life for a life*, he thought, amazed at the simplicity of the psychological equations in an area where he would have expected layer upon layer of murky Freudian complexity. Being born again allowed for no half-measures. He could not take from both existences, racking up debits in each, and therefore Gerald Mathieu had to be spared.

With the after-image of Silvia's full-breasted nakedness drifting in his vision, Dallen closed the cabin door behind him, but did not lock it. He turned towards the elevator. Two men—Renard and Captain Lessen—were approaching on the curved strip of deck between the cabins and the cargo well. As usual, they were engaged in heated argument, but Renard broke off on the instant of seeing Dallen and came straight to him, his gold-speckled face solemn.

"What were you doing in there?" he said directly. "It's a bit early for visiting, isn't it?"

Dallen shrugged. "Depends on how well people know each other."

"You're not fooling anybody, old son." Renard showed his bow of teeth as he waited for Lessen to sidle by him and get beyond earshot. His gaze was hunting over Dallen's face, and each passing second brought a change of his expression—amiable contempt, incredulity, alarm and dawning anger.

"If you'll excuse me," Dallen said, "I've got work to do." He tried to walk towards the elevator, but Renard detained him by placing a hand on his chest.

"You'd better listen to me," Renard said in a venomous whisper. "If I . . ."

"No, you'd better do the listening for once," Dallen said in matter-of-fact, conversational tones. "If you don't take your hand off me I'll hit you so hard that you'll be hospitalised for some time and may even die."

Renard was trying to form a reply when Lessen called to him in an aggrieved bark from the foot of the stair to Deck 4. Dallen ended the encounter by side-stepping Renard and walking to the elevator cage.

During the quivering descent to the bottom of the hold he indulged in a moment of satisfaction—perhaps Renard's trust in the universe was somewhat misplaced—and when the elevator stopped he went confidently to the lane which ended at Mathieu's stacks, taking the solvent sponge from his side pocket as he crossed the puddled floor. Sounds of movement nearby indicated that somebody was at work on the trays, but it was not until he had actually turned the corner

that Dallen realised that things were not what they
should be. High in the geometric jungle, amid the
scattered bars of light and shade, there were unexpected signs of movement.

Somebody was climbing to the top of Mathieu's
ladder.

In the instant of recognising the climber as Mathieu
himself, Dallen saw that he was in the act of reaching
for the topmost rung. With a despairing grunt, knowing he was too late to prevent the calamity, Dallen
hurled himself to the foot of the ladder and turned
his eyes upwards, bracing himself for what could
easily be a crippling impact.

He was greeted by the sight of Mathieu angled
nonchalantly outwards from the ladder, the slim plastic tube of his spray hose coiling down from his
waist. His weight was taken by his right hand gripping the top rung.

"What's going on down there?" Mathieu said, his
attention caught by the sudden movement.

"Nothing," Dallen assured him. "I slipped, that's
all." He backed up the story by pressing a hand to
his side as though nursing a strained muscle.

Mathieu descended at once. "Are you hurt?"

"It's nothing," Dallen said, experiencing a strange
mixture of emotions at being so close to the man who
had so profoundly affected his life. "But we ought to
get a mop and take away some of this surface water
before somebody really gets hurt." He rubbed his
side, excusing himself from the chore.

"I'll do it," Mathieu said compliantly. "I think
there's a kind of broom closet near the elevator." He
moved away and was lost to sight among the stacks.

As soon as he was sure of being unobserved, Dallen climbed Mathieu's ladder in a kind of vertical run, stopping when his face was level with the top rung. The light was less than ideal, but he could easily discern the frost-like coating of Pietzoff emulsion on the full length of the alloy tube, which meant that Mathieu should have received a fierce neural jolt as soon as his fingers had exerted pressure on the embedded crystals.

The only explanation Dallen could conceive was that the container he had stolen in Madison had come from a defective batch. Intrigued, momentarily forgetting the need for urgency, he lightly flicked the rung with a fingernail as a test.

The paralysing shock stabbed clear through to his feet.

His muscle control instantly disrupted, Dallen sagged and fell—then recovery came and he clung to the ladder, gasping with fright. He had almost dropped the whole way to the metal deck, a lethal twenty metres below, and had been saved only by the fact that his nail had served as a partial barrier to the Pietzoff's neural charge. And Mathieu was due to return at any second. Striving for full control over his body, Dallen inched upwards to regain the height he had lost. He squeezed the solvent sponge to activate it, wiped the top rung free of paint and got to the bottom of the ladder just as Mathieu appeared with a mop and bucket which could have been props from a period play.

"I love these high-tech solutions to the problems of space flight," he said, gamely cheerful as he set to work on the water-beaded deck, looking like a blond holo star making a bad job of playing a menial.

Dallen nodded, still slightly shaky, still baffled by his experience at the head of the ladder. By all the rules governing such things, Mathieu should have taken the big drop and hit the deck like a sack of bones. Was it possible that his right hand was an extremely lifelike prosthetic? Or was it merely, returning to the prosaic, that there had been an uneven distribution of crystals in the emulsion and Dallen had chosen the wrong place for his test? It hardly seemed likely, but it was the most acceptable explanation he could devise. Nobody was immune to Pietzoff.

"To think I gave up a good job for this," Mathieu said, mopping with casual efficiency. "I must have been crazy."

"Why did you pack it in? Was it Bryceland?"

"Bryceland? Mal-de-mayor?" Mathieu's eyes showed a cool amusement. "No, Garry, it was time for me to travel, that's all."

"I see." Again Dallen found it difficult to cope with the complexity of his reactions to Mathieu. The fact that the man had been spared a summary execution did not mean that he should be allowed to avoid the establishment's penalty for a major crime, but was it now too late to bring an accusation against him? What evidence would remain at this late stage? And, underlying everything else, why did the man himself seem to have changed? The difference was indefinable, but it was there. Gerald Mathieu had always given him the impression of being a vain gadfly, a hollow man, but now . . .

What's the matter with me? Dallen demanded of himself in bemused wonderment. *Why am I where Silvia isn't?*

He gave Mathieu a dismissive wave, walked back to the elevator and pressed the button for Deck 5. The cage made its customary shuddering ascent, passing layer after layer of miniature grassy plains, some in shadow, others bathed in artificial sunlight. By the time it halted at the ring deck Dallen had relegated Mathieu to the past. Nobody was about—the *Hawkshead's* crew spending virtually all their working hours in the outer hulls—and he was able to go without delay to Silvia's cabin. He was keyed-up and exhilarated as he pressed the door handle, so preternaturally alive that he could actually feel the subtle agitation of the ship's air. The handle refused to turn. Dallen tapped lightly on the door and stepped back a little, disappointed, when it was opened by the solidly androgynous figure of Doctor Billy Glaister.

"Silvia can't see you now," she announced triumphantly. "She's got to . . ."

"It's all right, Billy," Silvia said, appearing beside the other woman. In the short interval since Dallen had last seen her, she had brushed her hair back and had dressed in a black one-piece suit. She came out of the cabin, drew the door to, caught Dallen's arm and walked him towards the nearby stair.

"I'm sorry," she said. "Billy is inclined to be over-protective."

"Is that what you call it?"

"That's what it *is*." Silvia halted and gave him a very wise, very womanly smile. "When you cool down a little you'll be as glad as I am that she came back. This place isn't for us, Garry. Admit it."

Dallen glanced at the environment of smudged metal walls, stanchions and pipe runs. "It's idyllic."

She laughed and, in an unexpected gesture, raised the back of his hand to her lips and kissed it, somehow proving to him that all was well. "Garry, we'll reach Optima Thule in a day or two and as soon as Rick unloads his grass we'll be going on to Beachhead City, where there are good hotels, and where we'll have all the time we need to be together and make our plans. That's worth holding on for, isn't it?"

He looked down at her, unable to admit she was right, and forced himself to return her smile.

By the time another day had passed the ship had ceased most of its geometrical manipulations and was rapidly reaching a condition in which it could be perceived as a real object by outside observers. That, in turn, meant that human and inorganic watchers aboard the vessel could once again receive information from the normal space-time continuum.

Still shedding velocity at a rate of more than 1G, the *Hawkshead* took its bearings from Orbitsville's beacon network and began making course corrections, heading for Portal 36. The entrance had been assigned to it by the Optima Thule Science Commission because the surrounding terrain had never been contaminated by developers and therefore would yield the cleanest data in large-scale botanical experiments.

Professional space travellers rarely devoted any time to visual observation during final approaches to Orbitsville. At close ranges the vast non-reflective shell had always occluded half the universe, cheating the eye and confusing the intellect, creating the impression that *nothing* existed where in fact there was an impenetrable wall spanning the galactic horizon.

Thus it was that no member of the *Hawkshead's* crew was at a direct vision station when the vessel, guided by artificial senses, began groping its way towards Portal 36.

And thus it came about that it was Doctor Billy Glaister, habitual visitor to the ship's observation gallery, who discovered that Orbitsville had undergone a radical change.

The enigmatic material of its shell—black, immutable, totally inert in two centuries of mankind's experience—was suffused with a pulsing green light.

Chapter 17

The onset of weightlessness, gradual though it was, brought problems for Dallen.

In the early stages Cona had enjoyed her growing gymnastic ability, and had come dangerously close to hurting herself or Mikel during exuberant and ill-coordinated frolicking about the cabin. Then, as the *Hawkshead's* main drive neared total shutdown, the feeling of unnatural lightness progressed to become an outright falling sensation, and Cona's pleasure turned to fear. She clung to the frame of her bed, white-faced and whimpering, but resisted his efforts to secure her with the zero-G webbing. Mikel was more manageable, allowing himself to be tethered to his cot, and seemed less concerned with himself than with his toys' new tendency to float away in the air.

Dallen was retrieving a favourite model truck for him when a single chime from the communications panel signalled that the ship was entering the state of free fall. An uneasy lifting sensation in Dallen's stomach was accompanied by the sound of Cona retching.

Cursing himself for not having been prepared, he twisted towards her just in time to be caught in the skeins of yellowish fluid which had issued from her mouth. The acid smell of bile filled the cabin at once and Mikel began to sob.

Fighting to keep the heaving of his own stomach in check, Dallen drew a suction cleaner pipe out of the wall and used it to hunt down every slow-drifting globule. It took him another five minutes to clean himself and change his clothes, by which time his thoughts were turning away from his domestic troubles and towards truly macroscopic issues. As soon as the flickerwing drive had been deactivated the *Hawkshead* would have been able to enter radio contact with Orbitsville and request some kind of official explanation for what had happened to the shell. Presumably Captin Lessen already had the information, but—disturbingly—there had been no general announcement.

As one who had been born on Orbitsville, Dallen was anxious for that explanation. For him the sight of the inconceivable expanse of green fire, like a boundless ocean alive with noctilucence, had been the emotional equivalent of a severe earthquake. He had grown up on the Big O, had a primitive unquestioning faith in its permanence and immutability—and now the unthinkable was happening. Tendrils of new ideas were trying to worm their way into his mind and were making him afraid in a way that he had never known before, and it was a process he could not allow to continue.

As the minutes dragged by without any word from Lessen his unease and impatience grew more intense. Finally, and not without a twinge of guilt, he took a double-dose hypopad from a locker and placed it on his thumb. He went to Cona and, while overtly trying to make her more comfortable, pressed his thumb against her wrist and fired a cloud of sedative into her bloodstream. As soon as the drug had begun to take effect, rendering her drowsy and passive, he clipped the zero-G webbing across the yielding plumpness of her body and with a reassuring word to Mikel left the cabin.

The standard-issue magnetic stirrups he had fitted to his shoes made walking difficult at first, but by the time he reached the control deck he was moving with reasonable confidence. He found Lessen, Renard and a small group of the ship's officers gathered in front of the view panels, most of which showed luminous green horizons.

"You are not permitted in here," Lessen said to him at once, puffing his chest.

"Don't be ridiculous," Dallen said. "What the hell is going on down there?"

"I must insist that you . . ."

"Forget all that crap." Renard turned to Dallen with no sign of his former animosity. "This is really something, old son. We talked to Traffic Central and were told that the whole shell lit up like that about five hours ago. Before that, apparently, they had a lot of green meridians chasing each other round and round the surface, but now the illumination is general.

"And you notice the pulsing? They say it started off at about one every five seconds, but now it's up to nearly one a second." Renard grinned at the discrete views of Orbitsville, excited but seemingly untroubled.

It's all part of a process, Dallen thought, remembering his conversation with Peter Ezzati, his instinctive alarm feeding on Renard's lack of concern.

"What did they say about landing?" he said. "How does it affect us?"

"It doesn't. The word from the Science Commission is that the light doesn't affect anything. It's only light. Nothing is showing up on any kind of detector—except photometers, of course—so we just ignore it and go ahead with the landing. They say it's business as usual at all the other entrances."

"I don't like it" Lessen said gloomily.

Renard clapped a hand on his shoulder. "You don't have to like it, old son. All you have to do is fly my ship, so I suggest you get on with it without wasting any more valuable time. Okay?"

"If you don't mind," Dallen said, "I'd like to stay here and watch."

Renard made a sweeping gesture. "Be my guest."

Lessen swelled visibly, looking as though he would protest, then shrugged and with a practised zero-G shuffle moved to a central console. He keyed an instruction to the ship's computer. A few seconds later Dallen felt a faint tremoring in the deck and glowing jade horizons changed their attitudes as the secondary drive came to life. A short time later Portal 36 showed up on the forward screen, visible at first as a short dark line floating in the green luminescence. The line grew longer and thicker, developing into a widening ellipse which quite abruptly became a yawning aperture in the Orbitsville shell.

Dallen, in spite of knowing what to expect, felt a coolness coursing down his spine as he saw the blue—the impossible blue—of summer skies within the portal. For a moment he had an inkling of how Vance Garamond and his crew must have responded two centuries earlier when their flickerwing nosed its way into the shaft of sunlight radiating into space from the historic Portal 1. As the aperture became a perfect thousand-metre circle of azure, Orbitsville's interior sun swam into view and steadied at the centre.

Without quite knowing why, Dallen found himself having to blink to clear his vision. *I should have been with Silvia for this*, he thought, wondering if she was in the Deck 3 observation gallery.

"We're locked on station at an altitude of two thousand metres," Lessen said, glancing at Dallen to see if he was absorbing the information. "Beginning our descent now."

Dallen gave him a friendly nod, accepting the verbal peace offering, and watched the circle expand in a lateral screen. The descent was slow but continuous, and after fifteen minutes the separation between the ship and its destination had been reduced to tens of metres. Propelled and maintained in the docking attitude by computer-orchestrated thrusters, the *Hawkshead* was lowering itself towards one edge of the aperture. Sting-like grapples were projecting beneath the central hull, ready to clamp the ship in place. At any of Orbitsville's principal ports it would simply have been a matter of sliding into one of the huge docking cradles, but here it was necessary for the ship to find its own anchorage.

The final step, Dallen knew, would be to extend a transfer tube from an airlock and drive it through the diaphragm field which kept Orbitsville's atmosphere from spewing into space. He estimated that unloading the grass and seed samples could take no more than a day, and from that point on Silvia and he would be free to . . .

"I don't like this," Lessen announced, speaking

with a studied calmness which had the effect of momentarily stopping Dallen's heart. "Something doesn't add up."

As if to ratify the captain's statement, crimson and orange rectangles began to flash on the control console to the accompaniment of warning bleeps. Two of the ship's officers moved quickly to separate consoles and began tapping keys with quiet urgency. The deck stirred like an animal beneath Dallen's feet.

Renard cleared his throat. "Would somebody care to tell me what's going on? I do own this thing, you know."

"The thrusters are still delivering power," Lessen said. "But the ship has stopped moving."

"But all that means is . . ." Renard broke off, his coppery eyebrows drawing together.

"It means something is counteracting the thrust—and our sensors can't identify it. We have a separation of twenty eight metres between the shell and the datum line of the hull, so there is no physical obstruction, but we can't detect any field-type forces. I don't like it. I'm going to back off."

"There's no need for that," Renard said. "Push a bit harder."

The officer at the smaller console to Dallen's left raised his head. "There's no indication of any threat to the ship."

"I don't care," Lessen replied, strutting nervously like a dove. "Traffic Central said conditions were normal at all other portals, but they can't vouch for *anything* here. We'll have to dock somewhere else."

"Like hell we will," Renard said. "I've got an agricultural station and a team of bloody expensive research workers waiting for me down there. We're going in right here."

"You want to bet?" Lessen palmed a master control with showy vigour, asserting his authority.

Watching him closely, Dallen saw a look of spiteful triumph which lasted only a few seconds and vanished as the patterns of red and orange on the console changed. New audio alarms began an insistent buzzing. Dallen felt vulnerable and totally helpless as he tried in vain to interpret the various information displays around him. *It's all part of a process*, came the fugue-thought. *Orbitsville doesn't catch fire for nothing . . .*

"We're not gaining any altitude," the officer on his left said.

"Don't tell me things I already know," Lessen snapped, specks of saliva floating away from his lips. "Get me an explanation."

His subordinate's jaw sagged. "But . . ."

The protest was drowned in the clamour of yet another alarm, this time not the discreet warning emitted for the benefit of flight managers but a blood-freezing bellow which deliberately mimicked the obsolete klaxon to achieve maximum effect. Three blasts were followed by a recorded announcement:

"EMERGENCY! EMERGENCY! THE PRESSURE HULL HAS BEEN BREACHED. ALL PERSONNEL MUST PUT ON SPACESUITS WITHOUT DELAY. EMERGENCY!"

The message was repeated until Lessen killed the control deck speakers, and even then it could still be heard booming through the ship's lower compartments.

Dallen watched in sluggish disbelief as Lessen and the other officers went purposefully to lockers and opened them to reveal the dark-mawed golem-figures of spacesuits. Renard, too, seemed unable to move. Looking exasperated rather than alarmed, he stood with gold-freckled arms folded across his chest and gaped at the men who were struggling into suits.

"This isn't a safety drill," Lessen called out, his gaze fixed on Dallen. "You'd better get down to your cabin and look after your family. You'll find two suits in the emergency locker and a pressure crib for the boy."

"I don't feel any pressure drop," Dallen said, unable to shake off a dull obtuseness.

"That's right," Renard put in. "What's all the panic?"

Lessen, now fully suited except for the helmet, said, "I don't know what's happening, but I can assure you this is a genuine emergency. Something kept us from making contact with the shell, and when we tried to back off something else pushed us back down again. Both those forces are still at work. We're in a vice and something is winding hard on the handle—that's what the strain monitors say—and the hull is beginning to split."

"You don't seem all that worried to me," Renard accused.

"That's because *I'm* in my suit." Lessen gave Renard a malicious smile, refusing to cease feuding with him regardless of how dire he believed the situation to be.

Renard swore and ran towards the stairs in an ungainly slouch, his stirrups clacking noisily on the metal-cored deck. Dallen followed him as in a slow-motion dream. The emergency warning continued being broadcast on the lower decks, but he still had to contend with a sense of unreality.

Lessen had spoken of a mysterious "something" which, although invisible, was exerting a crushing force on the starship—but did it actually exist? Space was a sterile vacuum, not the habitat of mysterious entities who attacked ships. The *Hawkshead* was long past its best, and a more likely explanation for all that had occurred was that some of its systems had gone haywire. After all, the only evidence for the putative emergency was in information displays, and such devices could easily be . . .

Crang! Crip-crip-crip-crip-CRANG!

The sounds of a metal structure failing under stress came as Dallen was between Decks 4 and 5, and were followed by a slamming of unseen metal doors. This time his eardrums responded to a drop in air pressure, and now the emergency was real and now he was afraid. Truly afraid. Several people, Silvia among them, were gathered on Deck 5 helping each other with the unfamiliar task of putting on spacesuits. Giving Silvia a tense half-smile, Dallen slipped by them and went into his own cabin. Mikel, a toy vehicle clutched in each hand, was staring up at him uncertainly, but Cona was drowsing in her bed, oblivious to the disturbance.

"Everything is fine, son," Dallen said. "We're going to play a new game."

Keeping up a flow of reassuring patter, he opened a red-painted closet door and removed the pressure crib. It was an egg-shaped affair, with a transparency near one end, and had ample room for an infant. His hands trembling with haste, Dallen put Mikel inside it and closed the seals. Mikel gazed at him through the transparency, startled and reproachful, then began to cry. The sound reached Dallen by way of a speaker on the crib's life support control panel.

"I'm sorry, I'm sorry," he mumbled. "I promise it won't be for long."

He took an adult suit off its clips in the closet and began the more difficult task of getting Cona inside it. She was too drug-laden to offer any wilful resistance, but the sheer flaccidity and mass of her body, coupled with the lack of leverage due to zero gravity, hindered his every action. Within seconds he was sweating profusely. His co-ordination was impaired by anxiety, the constant aural battering from the PA system and Mikel's sobbing, plus the repetitious chanting in his head.

What's happening to the ship?

What's happening to Orbitsville?

When he finally got the suit closed around Cona and was reaching for the helmet she flung her head back in an involuntary spasm and struck him squarely on the bridge of the nose. Half-blinded by tears, he snorted out several quivering beads of blood and fitted Cona's helmet in place. She gave him a seraphic smile through its crystal curvatures, closed her eyes and lapsed back into sleep.

Grateful for the respite, he unclipped his own suit and was partially into it when the ear-punishing warning broadcast abruptly ceased. There was a moment of silence, then Lessen's voice was heard at a more tolerable volume. He spoke with irritating deliberation, either for clarity or in an effort to inspire confidence.

"This is Captain Lessen. The ship has suffered severe damage to its pressure hull. We have no alternative but to abandon the ship. Do not be alarmed. All crew and passengers should assemble immediately in the main airlock in the first quadrant of Deck 4. I repeat—do not be alarmed. You have only thirty metres of open space to cross, and there will be ropes to prevent anyone from drifting free. Go immediately to the main airlock in the first quadrant of Deck 4."

Dallen finished donning his suit and fitted the helmet in place, an action which activated the oxygen generator and temperature control systems. He had never worn a spacesuit before, except in safety drills, and felt oddly self-conscious as he tethered the crib to his belt and went to the cabin door with Cona awkwardly in tow. The other passengers had already left the ring-shaped Deck 5, but a crewman on his way to the next level saw Dallen's difficulty and came to his aid, taking responsibility for getting Cona up the narrow stair.

"Thanks," Dallen said. "I had to give her some heavy sedation."

"Save some for me," the man replied, his voice made disturbingly intimate by Dallen's helmet radio.

They reached the airlock and were impatiently counted into it by another suited crewman. The square chamber was large enough to hold the entire ship's company, all of whom seemed to be present judging by the babble of sound transmitted into Dallen's helmet. With the crib in his left arm and with Cona's bulk clamped to him by his right, he forced his way into the throng as a metal door slid shut behind him. The noise level increased abruptly as red lights began to glow on the walls and ceiling to indicate that the chamber's air was being bled off. More tremors coursed through the deck.

Suddenly Lessen's voice, augmented by his command transmitter, cut through the din. "Quiet, *please*! As you will have noticed, our suit radios operate on a common frequency. Stop all unnecessary talk immediately, otherwise . . . Well, I'm sure you can all see the need for speed and efficiency . . ." His voice was lost in a renewed burst of sound which was followed at once by a guilty near-silence.

Dallen became aware of the inner skin of his suit tightening itself against his limbs. A few seconds later a different set of lights began to flash on the outer wall of the chamber and he realised he was surrounded by vacuum. The uneasy novelty of the experience faded from his mind as the airlocks's outer doors parted to admit a shaft of sunlight beaming out of a breathtaking blue sky.

Until that moment Dallen had thought of the ship as hovering above the outer surface of Orbitsville—now, with a mind-wrenching shift of preception, he found himself peering *upwards*. The portal was a one-kilometre lake of blackness set amid Orbitsville's endless pampas, a circular well of stars, and anybody standing at its edge and looking downwards would see the *Hawkshead* as a huge submarine trapped below the surface. Inhabitants of the Big O lived with stars beneath their feet.

There was a multiple gasp of surprise from the assembled company as the airlock doors retreated fully and a section of the Orbitsville shell became visible at one side of the rectangular opening. It had an alien aspect, one never before seen by human eyes. In place of the inert and non-reflective darkness was a sheet of pale green radiance of an intensity which almost equalled that of the interior sky. The light was pulsing in a way that made the shell seem alive. Dallen stared at it, strickenly, filled with superstitious awe.

Orbitsville doesn't catch fire for nothing, he thought.

*It's all part of a . . . What frequency of pulsing did Renard
mention? Was it once a second? Surely what I'm seeing is
faster than once a second . . .*

There was a flurry of activity near the edge of the
airlock and the white-armoured figure of a man flew
from the ship towards the portal, a line uncoiling
behind him. He traversed the open space in only a
few seconds, but missed the portal's edge by a short
distance and Dallen saw him rebound from the invisible surface of the diaphragm field. He twisted
sideways, with the brief flaring of a reaction torch,
and managed to catch hold of a short ladder which
was clamped to the edge. He went up it, visibly
forcing himself through the field's spongy resistance,
and other men—dressed normally, moving freely in
Orbitsville's airy, sunlit warmth—were seen momentarily as they helped him to safety. There was a
spontaneous cheer from the watchers below.

He made it, Dallen thought bemusedly. *He made it,
and it was so easy, and everything is going to be all right,
after all . . .*

"That single line is enough for our purpose," Lessen
announced. "We will move along it hand-over-hand,
starting with the supernumeraries. Attach yourself to
the line with one of the short tethers you will find at
your waists. There will be no difficulty, so don't
worry. Now let's go!"

Dallen moved forward through the crowd with his
weightless human encumbrances, steadied and assisted
by willing hands. Ahead of him, figures were already
linked to and ascending the line. Captain Lessen,
distinguished by red triangles on his shoulders, was
positioned at the rim of the airlock, personally checking that each departing passenger was properly clipped

to the line. The direct sunlight glittered through crystal helmets and Dallen was able to recognise Silvia just as she set off across the void, closely followed by Renard. She went upwards towards their promised land with the fluid athleticism he would have expected.

The last passenger due to go before Dallen reached the bottom of the line was Gerald Mathieu. While his tether was being checked he gazed fixedly at Dallen, but without any sign of recognition, his face as colourless and immobile as marble. Without glancing into the starry gulf at his feet, he gripped the line and went up it slowly like a patient machine, barely advancing one hand beyond the other. Dallen tried to clip Cona on next, but Lessen prevented him.

"It'll be easier if you go first and bring your wife along behind you," Lessen said. "How is she?"

"Asleep on her feet."

"Just as well. Don't worry—we'll get her there."

"Thanks." With Lessen's help, Dallen linked himself to Cona at the waist, then connected both of them to the lifeline. The crib tethered to his waist was an additional complication, but the absence of weight and rope friction worked in his favour and he found it surprisingly easy to progress upwards with his two human satellites. Mikel had stopped sobbing and was staring placidly through the transparent panel of his ovoid. Dallen tried to concentrate all his attention on the sunlit blue sanctuary above, but there was a hungry blackness all around him and—even more distracting—the Orbitsville shell seemed to have grown brighter. The light from it was so intense as to interfere with vision, but the superimposed pulsing seemed to have increased its frequency to two or three times a second.

At this rate it will soon be continuous, Dallen thought, the first ice crystal of a new dread forming at the centre of his being. *What will happen then?*

He was now near the midpoint of the lifeline and was so close to Orbitsville that he could see the minutest details of what was happening at the edge of the portal. He saw Silvia and Renard, aided by other hands, force their way through the closure field and stand up, figures greatly foreshortened. Silvia removed her helmet immediately and he saw her breasts rise as she drew deeply upon Orbitsillve's pure air. She stood at the very rim of space, her face troubled as she looked downwards in his direction. Dallen tried to climb faster and made the discovery that he had caught up on Gerald Mathieu, who had stopped moving and was clenching the line with both fists.

"Mathieu! What the hell are you *doing*? Dallen positioned his helmet close to Mathieu's, looked closely into his face and recoiled as he saw the blind white crescents of the eyes and the fixed, frozen grin.

Captain Lessen's voice sounded clearly above a background hubbub. "What's happening up there?"

"It's Mathieu," Dallen replied. "I think he's dead. He's either dead or cataleptic."

"Christ! Can you push him ahead of you?"

"I'll try." Aware of the people below him on the line crowding nearer, Dallen gripped the nearer of Mathieu's gloved hands and tried to prise the rigid fingers open. Then he gasped in purest terror as the impossible happened.

The universe split into separate halves.

On Dallen's left, below him, was the partially sun-lit bulk of the ship, looming against the spangled backdrop of the galaxy. Down there he could see the red-glowing rectangle of the airlock, with spacesuited figures awaiting their turn to ascend the lifeline. Lessen was peering up at him, one hand raised to screen his eyes from Orbitsville's sun.

On Dallen's right, above him, was the inconceivable hugeness of Orbitsville itself. Up there, in one segment of his vision, he could see Silvia London and others outlined against a delicately ribbed blue sky. The remainder of his field of view on that side was taken up by the awesome green brilliance of the shell material, pulsing now at a frenetic rate, many times a second.

But in the centre, separating the two hemispheres of the universe, was a layer of utter blackness. It was narrow—barely wide enough to contain Mathieu, Dallen and his family—but he understood with an uncanny clarity that it stretched from one boundary of the cosmos to the other, that it was a dimension apart, at a remove from the normal continuum.

How . . .? Thought processes were painfully slow in the cryogenic chill that had descended over his brain. *How can I understand what I shouldn't be able to understand?*

A figure moved in the black stratum ahead of him, perhaps close, perhaps very distant. It was elongated, unlikely to be humanoid, and almost impossible to see—black sketched on black, a glass sculpture concealed in clear water.

Have no fear, Garry Dallen. Its voice was not a voice, but a thought implanted in Dallen's mind, perceived by him in the form of words, but cognisable beyond the limits of language. *I serve Life, and therefore you will not be harmed. Let it be known to you that I am a member of a race which has almost complete mobility in time and space. We are the ultimate embodiment of intelligent life. A meaningful comparison cannot be made, but you would say that we are farther ahead of humans in our evolution than humans are compared to, say, trilobites. We do not apply a generic name to ourselves, but a convenient noun for your use—fashioned according to your linguistic principles—is Ultan. I repeat that we Ultans are servants of Life, and there is no reason for you to be afraid.*

I can't help being afraid, Dallen responded. *Nothing could have prepared me for this.*

That is true. Chance has placed you in what may be a unique situation, but its duration will be very brief even by your standards—only a matter of seconds. All we require of you is that you do not break Gerald Mathieu's grip on the line or in any way force him towards the instrument you know as Orbitsville.

Why? What is happening? Even as he formulated the questions Dallen understood that he had already been altered by his mental contact with the other being. The mere fact of his being rational and self-controlled in the circumstances indicated that he had borrowed, no matter how temporarily, inhuman attributes from the dweller in the black dimension. He also understood that what his mind structure forced him to interpret as a human-style sequential dialogue was a near-instantaneous transfer of knowledge.

You are a fellow servant of Life, came the reply, *and the ethic demands that you be informed of matters concerning your existence.*

Be warned, Garry Dallen! The intervention by a different Ultan "voice" jolted Dallen, drawing his attention to another quadrant of the layer of blackness in which he was framed. As the second Ultan

invaded his mind he saw it moving, blackness modifying blackness, a barely perceptible presence.

*You are about to be given a false interpretation of the
Ethic,* the later arrival continued. *I urge you to reject it
and all its implications.*

*Wait! The human must now be allowed to reach his own
conclusion and act accordingly,* the first Ultan countered.

*I concede that, in our present situation of deadlock, no
other course is possible, but the Ethic requires that you
present him with facts only. You must not influence his
judgement.*

I am content to let reason be my advocate.

As am I—it can only be to my advantage.

Dallen sensed he was listening to implacable
enemies, beings who had long been engaged in some
awesome struggle and who were reluctant to arrange
an armistice. While their attention was concentrated
on each other he became aware of the figure of Mathieu
clamped rigidly by his hands to the line just above
him, and the essential mystery of what was happening grew deeper. The first Ultan wanted to prevent
Mathieu reaching Orbitsville—but *why?* What could
be the . . ?

Garry Dallen, an agreement has been reached. Dallen's
individuality was again lost in that of the entity which
had first made him aware of it. *The circumstances of our
meeting will be fully explained to you so that you may
choose to obey the Ethic in the full light of reason.*

*As a foundation upon which to build your understanding,
let it be known to you that the universe you inhabit is not
Totality. I can see, though, that you have already encountered ideas relevant to this subject, and therefore I shall use
compatible language.*

It is necessary for you to know that at the instant of the

Primal Event, known to you as the Big Bang, four universes are created. The one you inhabit—Region I in the terminology of some of your philosophers—appears to you to be constructed of normal matter and to have a positive time flow. It is counterbalanced by another universe—Region II—which from your viewpoint is composed of antimatter and has negative time flow. The Region II universe is moving farther and farther into your past, although its inhabitants naturally regard their matter as normal and their time flow as positive. They can never observe your universe, but they would conceive of it as being composed of antimatter and travelling into their past.

In addition, as postulated by some of your cosmogonists, there is Region III—a tachyon universe, which is rushing ahead of your universe in time; and there is Region IV—an anti-tachyon universe, which is fleeing into your past ahead of Region II. In the natural scheme of things, the four universes are not due to confront each other until the curvature of the space-time continuum brings them all together again—at which point there will be yet another Big Bang and a new cycle will begin again.

Dallen caught a memory-glimpse of a fantastic glass mosaic with its intricate petals. *I confirm that these ideas are not new to me, although I personally cannot cope with the concept of time itself being curved.*

The phrase "time itself" is at the heart of your difficulty, but it is enough for you to accept my statement. We Ultans are inhabitants of Region III, your tachyon universe, and our mobility in time and space gives us an overwhelming advantage in dealing with such concepts.

But I am more puzzled than before, Dallen responded. You have explained nothing.

The groundwork has to be extensive. It follows from what I have said that the universes created by each Big

Bang have to be closed universes. The attractive force in each universe has to be strong enough to recall its myriad galaxies from the limit of their outward flight, thus reassembling all the matter in the cosmos in preparation for the next Big Bang.

Were it not so, all the galaxies would continue to disperse. Eventually they would grow cold, and would die, and absolute darkness would descend over a cosmos which consisted of black cinders drifting outwards into infinite blackness. There would be no more cycles of cosmic renewal. Life would have ended for ever.

All that is clear to me. Dallen, in his altered state of consciousness, was aware of his infant son gazing with darkly rapt eyes from the interior of his egg-like crib. *But, still, nothing has been explained.*

The reason for our intervention in your affairs is this. After an unknown number of cosmic cycles an imbalance has developed. We have learned that Region II is an open universe. It cannot contract. It is destined to expand for ever, and without the contribution of its matter the nature of the next Big Bang will be radically altered. We foresee a catastrophic disruption of the cycle of cosmic renewal.

Dallen strove to concern himself with the fate of an anti-matter universe which had come into being perhaps twenty billion years earlier and had been travelling into the past ever since. *How could such an imbalance occur? If the mass of the Region II universe is equal to this one its gravitation must be . . .*

But gravity is not all, Garry Dallen. There is another and equally vital force which can augment and influence gravity, which can permeate and inform matter.

Dallen, transcending himself, made the intuitive leap. *Mind!*

That is so. The graviton and the mindon have a clear

*structural affinity, though it is one you are not yet equipped
to understand. There is a major difference, however. Gravity is an inherent, universal and unavoidable property of
matter—whereas mind arises locally and uncertainly, by
chance, when there is sufficient complexity in the organisation
of matter, and when other conditions are favourable. It then
propagates throughout galactic structures, enhancing the
chances of mind arising elsewhere, and at the same time
potentiating the action of gravity.*

*Most of your philosophers regard mankind as insignificant
in the cosmic scheme, but your race and a million others are
the cement which binds universes together. It is the thinker
in the quietness of his study who draws the remotest galaxies
back from the shores of night.*

So Karal London was on the right track! There was no
time for Dallen to be swamped by awe—the information exchanges continued at remorseless speed. *You
are telling me that mind did not flourish in the Region II
universe.*

*That is correct. The conditions were never favourable.
Even we Ultans cannot say why, but the probability of that
situation arising naturally is so low that we suspect a
malign intervention at an early stage of Region II's history.*

I protest! The second Ultan stirred in the blackness.
*I have allowed you uninterrupted access to the human, but
you abuse my forbearance by applying terms like malign to
the natural forces which shape Totality.*

*I apologise, but the important thing for Garry Dallen to
understand at this stage is that we have never regarded the
situation as irretrievable. We have taken steps to normalise
it.*

But that means . . . Dallen's mind was a sun going
nova. *Orbitsville!*

Yes. Orbitsville is an instrument, one which was designed

to attract intelligent life forms and to transport them back through time to the Region II universe. And the moment of departure is close.

No! The rapport between Dallen and the Ultan began to weaken, but he was still sufficiently in thrall to the near-invisible alien to react logically rather than emotionally. *It won't work! It can't make any difference—one sphere to an entire universe.*

We have deployed more than one sphere. To be sure of capturing a viable stock we constructed similar instruments in every galaxy in your universe. Each galaxy, depending on its size, has anywhere from eight to forty spheres, all of them in localities favourable to the development of intelligent life. Your race's discovery of Orbitsville was not entirely fortuitous.

A hundred billion galaxies, multiplied by . . ! Dallen faltered, numbed by immensity, as he tried to calculate the number of Orbitsvilles scattered through the universe.

The total may be large by human scales of magnitude, but the Region II universe has as many galaxies as this one—and all have to be seeded. The Ethic requires it.

WRONG! The forceful contradiction from the second Ultan disturbed and confused Dallen, further weakening the inhuman persuasive force of the first. He took one step nearer to his normal state of being, and as emotion began to pit itself against intellect his thoughts homed in on Silvia London. She was on Orbitsville. And Orbitsville, now pulsing so rapidly that the eye detected only a frenzied hammering on the retina, was about to depart . . .

Garry Dallen, you can see for yourself the fallacious nature of that interpretation of the Ethic. As the second Ultan forced itself upon Dallen's mind he detected it as an agitated swirling current of blackness. *I, in common with many of my kind, understand that we Ultans have no right to impose our will, our necessarily limited vision, upon the natural ordering of Totality. The imbalance between Regions I and II in the present cycle heralds drastic change—that is true—but it was change which produced us and all we know. Resistance to change is wrong. Totality must evolve.*

Why tell me? The psychic pressure on Dallen was becoming intolerable. *I'm only a man, and I have other . . .*

Chance has placed you in a unique situation, Garry Dallen. My forces are at a disadvantage in this part of this particular galaxy, and consequently I have had to proceed by stealth.

You have learned that Orbitsville is an instrument. To nullify it I, too, constructed an instrument—one which has only to make contact with the Orbitsville shell to be absorbed into it and denature it and lock it into the Region I continuum for ever. That instrument is the physical form of the being you knew as Gerald Mathieu.

I chose him because he wanted to terminate his own life, and because in your society he existed in circumstances which would allow him to travel to Orbitsville and approach it unobtrusively. When he killed himself by deliberately crashing his aircraft I recreated him—incorporating the physical modifications necessary for my purpose—and directed him to this point.

Unfortunately, his approach was detected and the preparations for the translation of this sphere into the Region II universe was speeded up. In addition, enormous energies are being directed against the body of Gerald Mathieu, paralysing it, counteracting my energies.

And now everything depends on you, Garry Dallen.

You are at the fulcrum, at the balance point of two of the greatest personalised forces in any universe, where neither can dominate you—where your own reason, will and physical strength can decide a cosmic issue.

Only seconds remain before the sphere is due to depart, but there is time for you to break Gerald Mathieu's hold on the line and propel his body into contact with the shell.

I, on behalf of the Ethic, charge you with that responsibility . . .

Dallen sobbed aloud as the two hemispheres of the divided universe clapped together.

His senses were returning to normal, but he knew that the entire confrontation with the Ultans had taken place between heartbeats. A confusion of gasps and startled cries from his suit radio suggested that the watchers in the *Hawkshead's* airlock had shared the experience to some extent. His three companions in the centre of the extra-dimensional episode knew least of all—Cona floating in her drug-induced torpor; Mikel in his starry-eyed incomprehension; Gerald Mathieu, dead but not dead, frozen to the line which snaked upwards to . . .

Dallen's breathing stopped as he saw that the shell material was a plane of green fire, its pulsations now so close together as to be almost beyond perception. The departure was imminent. There were no more reserves of time. Silvia was standing at the rim of the portal, leaning dangerously over the abyss, but restrained by Rick Renard's arms. Her lips were moving, forming words Dallen needed to hear, and her eyes were locked on his.

"Silvia," he shouted, surging up the line towards her. Mathieu's rigid body blocked the way, the blind face grinning into his. There had been talk of a great responsibility . . . of forcing the instrument that was Mathieu across those last few metres of space . . . but would take time . . . and there was no more time . . . the shell material was as bright as the sun . . . burning steadily . . .

No more fairness, Dallen screamed inwardly. *This is for ME!*

He unclipped himself from the lifeline, from his wife's inert figure, from his son's crib. He clawed his way around Mathieu's body, frantic with haste, and launched himself upwards toward the rim of the portal. Silvia extended her arms as if to catch him . . .

But Orbitsville vanished.

He had missed Silvia by a second, and now she was separated from him by a gulf of time equal to twice the age of the universe.

Dallen drew his knees up to his chin, closed his eyes, and went slowly tumbling into the newly created void.

Chapter 18

The headquarters of the London Anima Mundi Foundation had been set up a short distance south of Winnipeg for a number of reasons, an important one being administrative convenience. It was close to Metagov Central Clearing, the largest fragment of governmental machinery remaining on Earth, and therefore was at the centre of a pre-existing communications and transport network. A trickle of offworld traffic was coming in from the Moon, the various orbital stations and from Terranova, the single small planet which had been discovered before Orbitsville had relegated it to the status of a backwater. The level of traffic was barely enough to keep the facility alive, but that was seen as an important contribution to the Renaissance. The global picture was more encouraging than many futurologists would have predicted, but it would be a long time before there would be any reserve capacity in the technology-based industries.

Dallen was satisfied with the location for reasons of

his own, not the least being that the climate was often comparable to that of his native Orbitsville. There were days, especially in spring and fall, when the air flowing in across the high grasslands had an evocative steely purity which, taking him unawares, would cause him to tilt his head and search the skies as though he might see in them the pale blue watered silk archways of his childhood. And even in midsummer, when the temperatures were higher than he would have preferred, the air was lively and had a freshness he did not associate with Earth.

This was a good place to bring up my son, he thought as he waited for the breakfast coffee to percolate. *Good as any place you would find*.

It was a diamond-clear morning—one of a seemingly endless succession of fine mornings in that summer—yet he was acutely conscious of the date as he moved about the familiar environment of the kitchen. August 25, 2302. Only nine years had passed since Orbitsville had departed for another universe, but it had been *two whole centuries* since an exploration ship had slipped away from the Earth-Moon system heading for unknown space. Now the *Columbus* was fully stored and ready to spiral out of Polar Band One to test itself against sun-seeded infinities, and the date would be one for the history books.

The thought of books drew Dallen from the kitchen and into the pleasant, long-windowed room he used as a study. One wall featured a custom-built rosewood case which held exactly four hundred literary works, many with antique bindings which proclaimed them to be early editions. In the centre of the case, glazed and framed, was the handwritten reading list which had been the basis of the collection. Dallen smiled as he ran his gaze over the display, taking a wholesome and pleasurable pride in having read every volume, from Chaucer right through to the major 23rd Century poets. His brain, conditioned by nine years of schooling in total recall techniques, effortlessly recreated the circumstances in which he had recovered the list . . .

For protracted aching minutes after the disappearance of Orbitsville the group of people who had tried to enter Portal 36 had been too stricken to think coherently or act constructively. Dallen remembered continuing his slow-tumbling fall towards the sun, his mind a chaotic battleground for alien concepts and a crushing sense of personal loss, unable to care much about whether he was going to be lost or saved. He had been thousands of metres away from the *Hawkshead* before the crewman dispatched by Captain Lessen had overtaken him and jetted them both back to safety. The ship's pressure skin, abruptly released from an invisible vise, had resealed itself within its elastic limits and the air losses were no longer a matter of urgency.

In the days that followed Dallen had been able to lose himself in hard work, because—once the incredible truth about the sphere had been accepted—there remained the practical business of the return to Earth.

Many starships, ranging in type from bulk carriers to passenger vessels, had been left in a vast circle around the sun when Orbitsville had vanished from the normal continuum. Forming part of the same circle, but in much larger numbers, had been an even wider variety of interportal ships, many of which had been en route when their destinations had ceased to exist. In some extreme cases, maintenance workers on exterior port structures had been left floating in space, clinging to sliced-off sections of docking cradles.

The salvage operation had been facilitated by the fact that everything left behind was in a stable and tidy orbit around the sun, and was also provided with stellar heat. As a preliminary to the retreat to Earth, all personnel with only spacesuits or unpowered habitats to keep them alive had been located and rescued by small craft. Next, all ships—large and small—had gathered in a single orbiting swarm, and the interstellar vessels had taken on board every human being left in that region of space. That stage of the operation had been complicated by the arrival of twelve ships from Earth and one from Terranova, all of which had been locked in warp transfer at the time of the disappearance, but the problems had been mostly concerned with credibility and had eventually been resolved. The thesis that Orbitsville no longer existed, although astonishing, was remarkably easy to demonstrate.

The logistics of assembling the return fleet had been such that Dallen had plenty of time to rescue his family's possessions from the condemned *Hawkshead* and transfer them to an aging but grandiose passenger liner, the *Rosetta*, in which they had been assigned a suite. And it had been while repacking some oddments that he had found the reading list folded and tucked into a rarely-used tobacco pouch. Cona had prepared it for his benefit three years earlier. It detailed four hundred books she regarded as important and which she had urged him to read.

"That's purely for starters," she had said, smiling. "Just to give you some idea of where you came from and where you ought to be going."

The old Dallen had refused the intellectual gift, inflicting unknown pain by not trying even one of the suggested books, but the new Dallen had been determined to make amends. Standing there in the special sunlight of that special morning, he touched the oiled wood of the bookcase, recognising and respecting all that remained to him of his former wife. The body which had once belonged to Cona was now inhabited by a cheerful and uncomplicated young woman who had a mental age of about thirteen and whose home was on a nearby farm owned by the Foundation. Belatedly accepting his former physician's advice, Dallen had renamed her Carol and used the name automatically in his thoughts.

He went to visit Carol once a month and occasionally they would go horseback riding together, and he was always glad that their relationship, although pleasant, was cool and undemanding. Carol treated him as she would an uncle, sometimes enjoying his visits a lot and at others showing impatience over being dragged away from the stables. The active farming life had pared her figure down, taking years off her apparent age, with the result that when Dallen saw her from a distance there was little to remind him of his former wife—*Cona Dallen doesn't live here any more*—and he had learned that all grief has to fade.

"Coffee in five minutes," he shouted, hearing the first subdued *thump* from the old-style percolator in the kitchen. He arranged settings for three people at the breakfast bar, then returned to the study and sat down at his desk. The computer displayed his job notes for the day, but he found it hard to concentrate on the symbols when the lawns and shrubs beyond

his window were glowing with a phosporescent
nostalgic brilliance and the *Columbus* was circling up
there beyond the atmosphere, making ready for deep
space. Dallen reached for his pipe and, while filling
it, allowed his thoughts to drift back over the previous
nine years.

Dwelling in the past was psychologically inadvisable
for most people, but in his case it had literally become a way of life, a profession. Project Recap had
been set up within weeks of his return to Earth after
the Orbitsville departure, with Dallen as a principal
director. In the early stages all but three of the thirty-
four men and women who had witnessed and been
affected by the seminal encounter with the Ultans had
been part of the team, each making a unique contribution to the collective memory. The ineffable moment
of wordless, mind-to-mind contact had been shared
by all, but the common experience had been inter-
preted by individuals in different ways, modified by
their intelligence, outlook and education.

Holorecordings of the event—with their hazy images of black entities shimmering in blackness—had
proved to the rest of humanity that *something* had
happened, but it had been the very diversity of the
participants' reactions which had finally eliminated
all theories about mass hysteria. Doctor Glaister, for
example, with her background in particle physics,
had emerged from the experience with recollections
which varied a great deal from Dallen's in some places,
especially where the "dialogue" had touched on the
relationship between mindons and gravitons. The detailed insights she had received—"cameos of cold logic,
engraved in permafrost, with the black ice of eternity
showing through" was how she once described them—

revitalised her entire field of learning, in spite of the fact that only one in a thousand of its workers had not been translated into the Region II universe.

The effect had been similar, though to a lesser extent, with some technical and engineering experts of the *Hawkshead's* crew, and it was largely as a result of their subsequent work that the exploration ship *Columbus* would be able to fly at close to tachyon speeds, bringing the core of the galaxy within mankind's reach. Other members of the same group had formed a cadre of inspired technocrats who, with material assistance from Terranova, were playing a vital role in the Renaissance.

The after-effects of the unique encounter had not been uniformly beneficial, however. The three men who had not been able to participate in Project Recap had been jolted by their experience into a profound autism which still gave little sign of abating. Dallen himself, prime target for the Ultans' psychic energies, had been disturbed for weeks, prone to nightmares and loss of appetite, alternating between periods of torpor and hyperactivity. When he had learned that his work for the Project would involve repeated and full-scale mental regression to the encounter he had at first refused to cooperate in any way, and only gradually had overcome his instinctive fears. There had also been the problem of his disbelief in the essential proposition.

The central idea was that the Ultans could be used retrospectively as a kind of sounding board for scientific and philosophical beliefs to be specially implanted in Dallen's mind. By drug-intensified hypnotic regression he would be able to meet the superhuman entities again and again, recreating a special state of consciousness, continuing to harvest or corroborate knowledge, to glean and scavange until the law of diminishing returns made the exercise pointless.

His scepticism had gradually faded when he discovered he had already, in association with Billie Głaister, helped change men's thinking about no less a question than the ultimate fate of the universe. Cosmologists had never been able to find enough mass in the universe, even with allowance for black holes, to guarantee that it was closed and therefore cyclic. The best they had been able to hope for was the Einstein-de Sitter model of a marginally open or flat universe, one which barely expanded but would go on doing so for ever. However, the mindon/graviton component imposed a positive curvature on spacetime, promising an infinite sequence of Big Squeezes and Big Bangs. The cosmological timescales were such that Dallen could feel little personal concern, but he could see that a cyclic universe was more pleasing to philosophers.

Of much greater interest to him were the questions posed by the mindon science of the Renaissance. The very fact that it not only accepted personal immortality, but had it as a cornerstone, made it unlike any scientific discipline that had gone before. It was exuberant, optimistic, mystical, life-centred, full of wild cards, boasting as one of its creeds a statement hypnotically retrieved by Dallen from the Ultan encounter: *It is the thinker in the quietness of his study who draws the remotest galaxies back from the shores of night.*

Dallen liked to regard himself as an integral part of the universe, and he savoured the irony in the way in which human beings, who had until recently accepted a life expectancy of some eighty years, were

now debating their prospects of surviving the next
Big Bang as mindon entities.

"Science used to be preoccupied with tacking on
more and more decimal places," a colleague told him.
"Now we add on bunches of zeroes."

It had been that moral buoyancy, the powerful
life-enhancing elements of mindon science, which had
given Dallen the necessary incentive to join Project
Recap. To the world at large the demanding aspect of
his work had been the mental wear and tear caused
by the periods of intensive study of abstruse subjects
followed by regressions and the subsequent debriefings.
Dallen had found the process intellectually harrowing,
but the principal strain had been emotional—for it
entailed his losing Silvia London time after time. One
system of thought demanded that he regard her as
having lived out her life billions of years before the
oldest stars in the universe were formed; but in
another—the one which was instinctive and natural
to Dallen—she was vitally alive, separated from him
only by some malevolent trick of cosmic geometry.
And both systems had exacted their due of bitter
tears.

For months after the premature death of his mother
Dallen had been haunted by fantastic dreams in which
she was still alive, and on his awakening his grief had
returned with almost its original force. A similar
sequence occurred with Silvia. Over and over again,
in the slow-motion quasi-existence of hypnotic regression, he saw her reaching her arms towards him as he
flew upwards to the edge of the portal. He saw her
tears and was able to read the words on her lips: *I
love you, I love you, I love you* . . .

The subsequent dreams were varied. In some he

reached the portal and forced his way through the diaphragm field in time to voyage with Silvia into the Region II universe, in others she remained behind with him in the normal continuum, but—dreams being what they are, with their own laws and logics—the one that troubled him most was the one which took the threads of reality and wove them into the most fantastic, least realistic pattern. Dallen had it on the authority of the Ultans themselves that there were anywhere from eight to forty of their titanic spheres in the Milky Way system. He had also been told that the sphere known to mankind as Orbitsville had been forced to leave earlier than scheduled—which meant that the others were still located in various arms of the galaxy, still making their unhurried preparations to depart for another continuum. In the dream Dallen sailed out on a tachyon ship, found one of the remaining spheres, and entered it just in time to be transported to a Region II galaxy. And in the dream he quit the second sphere and flew with magical ease and certainty to Orbitsville, and was reunited with Silvia.

To the dreaming mind such epic flights, far from seeming preposterous, are perfectly natural and normal, and that was the vision Dallen's unconscious elected to repeat most, its poignancy magnified by the very factors which divorced it from reality. At first he expected the dream to retain its full power, then he realised that his grief over the loss of Silvia was following the merciful and inevitable course of all passions. Pain softened into sadness, sadness mellowed into resignation, then it came to Dallen that he was truly a different person. The change had begun when he had finally acknowledged that he *deserved* to love Silvia and be loved by her in return, and it had been accelerated by his having, for the first time in his life, work he found absorbing and worthwhile.

Cosmogony and cosmology were only part of Project Recap's domain—there was the subject of the Ultans themselves. As the one who had had the closest mental contact with the enigmatic beings, Dallen was assigned the position of leading expert in the brand-new field of study, but he was well aware of his human inadequacies. In common with all other members of the original encounter group, when he tried to empathise with the Ultans, to penetrate their minds, all he divined was an overpowering sense of coldness. For Dallen the feeling was reinforced by his recollection of the icy calmness of the aliens, of their dispassionate reliance on logic as they tried to influence him mere seconds before the Orbitsville departure.

There were arguments and counter-arguments, all based on speculation. Perhaps the humans, like receivers tuned to a single radio frequency, had been oblivious to a wide spectrum of telepathic transmission. The Ultans, it was reasoned, must be capable of human-like feelings because they were engaged in conflict and were not above using subterfuge. On the other hand, perhaps they had betrayed no trace of emotion because—and this was the argument which had dismayed many people—the fate of Orbitsville, so important in human terms, was infinitesmal in the Ultan scheme of existence. After all, what did it matter about one sphere when more than a million times a million of them had been deployed in an olympian struggle to shape a future universe? Nothing could be deduced about the probable outcome of that struggle, nor about the super-dimensional symmetry of the next Big Bang, using the fact that Orbitsville was now located in Region II. Orbitsville was too insignificant, a single grain of sand on a storm-swept shore . . .

"This is the last call for coffee," Dallen bellowed. "If nobody shows up I'm having the lot."

There was a scuffling and the sound of laughter from the direction of the bedrooms, and a second later Nancy Jurasek and Mikel jostled their way into the kitchen. Nancy was an engineer with the Industrial Reclamation Office in Winnipeg. She devised ways of reactivating municipal services for the benefit of people drifting back into the cities from the old independent communes. She was dark-haired and vivacious, and in the two years she had been living with Dallen had built an excellent relationship with Mikel, playing the role of substitute mother or sister when required, but in general simply being herself. One of her most valuable contributions had been in bringing out the irreverent and fun-loving side of Mikel's nature, characteristics he had had little chance to develop in the cloistered atmosphere of the Foundation.

Mikel accepted a beaker of coffee from Dallen, sipped it and made a grimace of distaste. "The thing I look forward to most about the *Columbus*," he said earnestly, "is getting a break from Dad's coffee."

Dallen pretended to be hurt. "I was going to make a big flask of it to send with you."

"There's a law against shipping toxic wastes."

Mikel dodged a playful swipe from Dallen, sat down at the breakfast bar and began to eat toast. Although not quite eleven years old, he was taller than Nancy and had an unruly appetite. He also had a prodigious talent for mathematics and physics, and had fully earned his place on the *Columbus* science team. Dallen's feelings had been mixed when he was giving his permission for Mikel to go on the exploratory flight. His instinctive parental feeling was that the boy was too young to leave home and venture into space, even for two months, but in his regressions to the Ultan encounter he had had repeated glimpses of the infant Mikel's face, the eyes blackly luminous as they gazed from the interior of the ovoid crib. It was something he had never discussed with the others, and there were no relevant criteria, but Dallen could half-believe that his son had been born again in that moment, a true child of space, with a mind/brain complex which by a freak of destiny had been readied by Gerald Mathieu for a singular congress with the Ultans, a tabula rasa for alien stylii.

If that were the case, if Mikel had been uniquely prepared to lead new generations to the stars, it could be seen as a curious atonement for Mathieu's original crime. Thinking back to the awesome events nine years in the past, Dallen could find in himself no residue of the hatred which had dominated and disfigured a part of his life. When Gerald Mathieu had been reeled back into the *Hawkshead's* airlock he had been found to be dead, with no apparent physiological cause. His body had been consigned to the Orbitsville sun and it was as though Dallen's negative emotions had gone into that stellar crucible with it. Now the entire episode seemed like a dream, and all that remained to him from it were echoes of feelings, stray reflections of things that might have been.

Had the group which reached the portal also been in mental contact with the Ultans? Dallen posed himself the familiar, unanswerable questions as he sipped his coffee. *Were they telepathically appraised of their situation? Or had they been mystified when the ship and all connected to it had ceased to exist and strange constellations had flared beneath their feet? Had Silvia and Renard had children? What was she doing at that very moment, forty billion years ago in a different universe?*

"You seem a little quiet this morning," Nancy said. "Worried about Mikel?"

"No, the *Columbus* is a good ship," Dallen replied, glancing at his son who was still munching toast. "And he'll only be gone for two months."

"Two months for *this* trip," Mikel said, his eyes growing darkly rapt in the way that Dallen remembered so well. "In that time we'll travel farther than anybody has ever done, but that's just for starters. Soon we'll be able to do anything . . . cross the galaxy . . . go hunting for Ultan spheres . . ."

Nancy gave a delighted laugh. "Dream on, child!"

"It isn't as far-fetched as you might think," Mikel said, a solemn expression appearing on his face as he tapped into his prodigal's intellect. "Here's a possible scenario for you to consider. We know that the Ultans put a minimum of eight spheres into this galaxy, and we were also told that they selected locations favourable to the development of intelligent life. Well, when we have improved our knowledge of this region of space sufficiently we will be able to decide what characteristics it has that make it a good site for a sphere. Then we can search for other similar areas in the galaxy and track down other spheres."

"Easy as pie," Nancy said scornfully, "but what happens if you bump into the Ultans themselves?"

Dallen enjoyed the way in which Nancy and Mikel

were consciously playing word games, building an edifice of purest fantasy, but at some point they had begun to stray close to the chimerical never-never land of his old recurrent dream. He found himself oddly intent as he waited for the boy's answer.

"But that's what we'd be *trying* to do," Mikel said. "The spheres themselves are of no value to us. What we want is to find the Ultans, study them, learn from them, communicate with them."

"And what great message would you pass on?"

Mikel frowned, and for an instant his boyish features were overprinted with the face of the man he was to become. "For one thing—I'd let them know we don't appreciate being treated like cattle."

Dallen turned away thoughtfully, realising he was almost afraid of his own son, then it came to him that he was listening to the voice of a new age. The Orbitsville phase had ended. In future when men set out to straddle the galaxy they would be searching for more than just areas of grass on which to pitch their tents. Equipped with superb tachyon ships, girded with mindon science, consciously immortal, they would have aims which could be incomprehensible to men of Dallen's generation. But there was nothing wrong with that, he reasoned. It was a sign that mankind was on the move again, and he should feel nothing but gladness that he had contributed to the process of vital change.

In the afternoon Dallen stood with one arm around Nancy at the Winnipeg spaceport, watching the shuttle carry his son up to an orbital rendezvous with the *Columbus*. There was no denying the sadness he felt over parting with the boy, at the idea of Mikel spending his eleventh birthday farther from Earth than men had ever been before. But the transcendental mood of the morning still lingered, sustaining him as the shuttle dwindled to a silver point and disappeared in the wind-scoured blueness of the sky.

Ultans, he thought, *we'll see you around*!

DAW
Presenting C. J. CHERRYH

Two Hugos so far—and more sure to come!

The Morgaine Novels
- [ ] GATE OF IVREL   (#UE1615—$1.75)
- [ ] WELL OF SHIUAN   (#UE1699—$2.75)
- [ ] FIRES OF AZEROTH   (#UE1925—$2.50)

The Faded Sun Novels
- [ ] THE FADED SUN: KESRITH   (#UE1950—$3.50)
- [ ] THE FADED SUN: SHON'JIR   (#UE1889—$2.95)
- [ ] THE FADED SUN: KUTATH   (#UE1856—$2.75)

- [ ] DOWNBELOW STATION   (#UE1828—$2.75)
- [ ] MERCHANTER'S LUCK   (#UE1745—$2.95)
- [ ] PORT ETERNITY   (#UE1769—$2.50)
- [ ] WAVE WITHOUT A SHORE   (#UE1646—$2.25)
- [ ] SUNFALL   (#UE1881—$2.50)
- [ ] BROTHERS OF EARTH   (#UE1869—$2.95)
- [ ] THE PRIDE OF CHANUR   (#UE1694—$2.95)
- [ ] CHANUR'S VENTURE   (#UE1989—$2.95)
- [ ] SERPENT'S REACH   (#UE1682—$2.50)
- [ ] HUNTER OF WORLDS   (#UE1872—$2.95)
- [ ] HESTIA   (#UE1680—$2.25)
- [ ] VOYAGER IN NIGHT   (#UE1920—$2.95)
- [ ] THE DREAMSTONE   (#UE1808—$2.75)
- [ ] THE TREE OF SWORDS AND JEWELS   (#UE1850—$2.95)

NEW AMERICAN LIBRARY
P.O. Box 999, Bergenfield, New Jersey 07621

Please send me the DAW BOOKS I have checked above. I am enclosing
$_____ (check or money order—no currency or C.O.D.'s).
Please include the list price plus $1.00 per order to cover handling
costs.

Name _____

Address _____

City _____ State _____ Zip Code _____
Please allow at least 4 weeks for delivery

DAW

DAW BRINGS YOU THESE BESTSELLERS BY
MARION ZIMMER BRADLEY

☐ CITY OF SORCERY	UE1962—$3.50
☐ DARKOVER LANDFALL	UE1906—$2.50
☐ THE SPELL SWORD	UE1891—$2.25
☐ THE HERITAGE OF HASTUR	UE1967—$3.50
☐ THE SHATTERED CHAIN	UE1961—$3.50
☐ THE FORBIDDEN TOWER	UE1894—$3.50
☐ STORMQUEEN!	UE1951—$3.50
☐ TWO TO CONQUER	UE1876—$2.95
☐ SHARRA'S EXILE	UE1988—$3.95
☐ HAWKMISTRESS	UE1958—$3.50
☐ THENDARA HOUSE	UE1857—$3.50
☐ HUNTERS OF THE RED MOON	UE1968—$2.50
☐ THE SURVIVORS	UE1861—$2.95

Anthologies

☐ THE KEEPER'S PRICE	UE1931—$2.50
☐ SWORD OF CHAOS	UE1722—$2.95
☐ SWORD AND SORCERESS	UE1928—$2.95

DAW

A GALAXY OF SCIENCE FICTION STARS!

TIMOTHY ZAHN The Blackcollar	UE1959—$3.50
JOHN STEAKLEY Armor	UE1979—$3.95
SHARON GREEN Mind Guest	UE1973—$3.50
M.A. FOSTER The Gameplayers of Zan	UE1993—$3.95
C.J. CHERRYH Forty Thousand in Gehenna	UE1952—$3.50
SUZETTE HADEN ELGIN Native Tongue	UE1945—$3.50
NEAL BARRETT, JR. The Karma Corps	UE1976—$2.75
JO CLAYTON The Snares of Ibex	UE1974—$2.95
ROBERT TREBOR An XT Called Stanley	UE1865—$2.50
JOHN BRUNNER The Jagged Orbit	UE1917—$2.95
PHILIP WYLIE The End of the Dream	UE1900—$2.25
LEE CORREY Manna	UE1896—$2.95
DAVID J. LAKE The Ring of Truth	UE1935—$2.95
E.C. TUBB Symbol of Terra	UE1955—$2.75
ROGER ZELAZNY Deus Irae	UE1887—$2.50
PHILIP K. DICK Ubik	UE1859—$2.50
WILLIAM L. CHESTER Kioga of the Wilderness	UE1847—$2.95
M.A.R. BARKER The Man of Gold	UE1940—$3.50
BOB SHAW The Ceres Solution	UE1946—$2.95
FREDERIK POHL Demon in the Skull	UE1939—$2.50

DAW

The adventures of Dray Prescot on the planet Kregen of the double-star Antares is the greatest interplanetary series of its kind since Edgar Rice Burroughs and Edward E. Smith stopped writing. Now the greatest of these novels, a powerful trilogy, has been specially reprinted by popular demand.

THE KROZAIR CYCLE

Covers by Michael Whelan! Interior Illustrations!

☐ **THE TIDES OF KREGEN**   (UE2034—$2.75)
  Illustrated by Michael Whelan.

☐ **RENEGADE OF KREGEN**   (UE2035—$2.75)
  Illustrated by Jack Gaughan.

☐ **KROZAIR OF KREGEN**   (UE2036—$2.75)
  Illustrated by Josh Kirby.

As told by Dray Prescot himself to Alan Burt Akers.

Heroic fantasy at its very best!
